TO DREAM

A Broken Roads Romance

Other books by Carolyn Brown:

The *Broken Roads Romance* Series:

To Believe
To Trust
To Commit

The *Drifters and Dreamers Romance* Series:

Morning Glory
Sweet Tilly
Evening Star

Love Is
A Falling Star
All the Way from Texas
The Yard Rose
The Ivy Tree
Lily's White Lace
That Way Again
The Wager
Trouble in Paradise
The PMS Club
The Dove

TO DREAM

•

Carolyn Brown

AVALON BOOKS
NEW YORK

Pro

Published by Thomas Bouregy & Co., Inc.
160 Madison Avenue, New York, NY 10016

Library of Congress Cataloging-in-Publication Data

Brown, Carolyn, 1948–
    To dream / Carolyn Brown.
        p. cm.
    ISBN 978-0-8034-9954-6
    1. Oklahoma—Fiction.   I. Title.
    PS3552.R685275T583 2009
    813'.54—dc22
                            2009007600

PRINTED IN THE UNITED STATES OF AMERICA
ON ACID-FREE PAPER
BY HADDON CRAFTSMEN, BLOOMSBURG, PENNSYLVANIA

In memory of my grandparents,
Herman and Edna Gray

Chapter One

Greta Fields' life did not flash before her when she braked hard and jerked the steering wheel to the left. No instant replays of all the good times, bad times, boring times, or even bah-humbug days visualized in front of her. What did fill the car as it spun out of control was the memory of her father's deep booming voice yelling at her the last time she'd wrecked her car, or was it the time before that? Vance Fields' loud voice reminding her that her chances were gone as the air bag exploded and she realized that she'd just used up her sixth life if she'd been a cat. She fought the air bag, loosened the seat belt and crawled out of the car, only to slip in the mud, break the heel off a brand-new pair of bright red Prada pumps, and fall flat on her back. While she struggled to stand up that same man who'd riled her at her

1

brother's wedding reception the night before stomped across the road. He kept screaming something about a bull and her stupidity with a few choice words thrown in about her being irresponsible and rich but that she wasn't getting away with killing his bull. He didn't even offer to help her find the heel she'd broken off her shoe or ask if she had been harmed. He was more interested in a bull than her. Her first impression of him had been right the night before. He wasn't anything but a small-town redneck cop.

Her life did zoom past when she was led into the judge's chambers on Sunday morning after spending the night in jail. Her black hair hung in limp strands and still had mud hanging in spots despite her efforts. The jail sweat pants and T-shirt were cheap and scratchy against her skin. She felt grimy and dirty and wanted a bath. Looking like she'd been the only chicken at a coyote convention, she took a deep breath and straightened her backbone with dignity. Even with day-old mascara smeared across taupe-colored eye shadow, she wouldn't let anyone get the best of her. She'd bluff even if the acrid taste of defeat filled her soul. Just where in the devil were her father and mother?

Bookcases covered with glass doors covered three walls of the small room. An enormous mahogany desk with family pictures on one end and an old-fashioned black desk phone on the other claimed a good chunk of the middle. Greta took a deep breath and smelled furniture polish, cigar smoke, and a faint whiff of something floral. She looked around until she found one of those plug-in room fresheners on the wall right beside the light switch. This judge couldn't be mean and hateful, not with two cute little girls' pictures on his desk and a plug-in room freshener. He was an old softy for sure. He'd be lenient and give her one more chance. Her father would come and pay her bail, like always. He'd yell for a while, telling her that twenty-five was old enough to be a heck of a lot more responsible and tomorrow they'd go shopping for another car. She thought she might like a blue one this time.

The door opened and a tall thin man who looked like Abraham Lincoln without a beard held the door for Etta Cahill. He wore a dark suit and a red tie and was all gangly arms and legs. He motioned for Etta to sit in a chair. He sat down behind the desk and opened a file.

Greta remained standing. She heard someone else close the door and figured it was the bailiff who'd led her from the jail, across the lawn, and into the court house. A nice enough man but not prone to talking, except to tell her she'd better not make the judge mad or learn to like the cell where she'd spent the night. According to him the only thing meaner than Judge Amos was a constipated cougar with an ingrown toenail. He was bluffing, trying to scare her, but it didn't work. She'd never seen a man yet she couldn't tame in thirty seconds.

Why on earth was Etta Cahill there? She was Roseanna's grandmother and Roseanna was her twice-despised sister-in-law. She'd remarried Greta's brother

Friday night. To Greta's way of thinking it was the second time Trey had made a mess of his life, and both times to the same woman. It might take a few years but Trey would come to his senses when the bloom was off the honeymoon. Not that Greta didn't admire Roseanna. She was a strong, admirable woman. She just wasn't the right one for Trey. He belonged in a corporate office, not on the back side of a ranch in a double-wide trailer with a rancher-slash-tracker for a wife.

Greta wished the judge would motion for her to sit in the other chair. Her knees were beginning to sag as she waited for the lecture. Etta sat easy in the chair while the judge reviewed the file. She was a gray-haired grandmotherly type lady but there was a no-nonsense look about her. She wore jeans and a T-shirt with some sort of cruise ship logo. Oh, yes, Greta remembered the stories from the wedding.

Etta and her friend, Roxie Hooper, had gone on a cruise during the summer. It all started last year when Roseanna and Trey, Greta's older brother, divorced. He'd been kidnapped a few months after the divorce and Greta was sent to see if Roseanna, a former cop and tracker, could rescue him. That part had gone well, but her stupid brother had fallen in love with Roseanna all over again and talked Etta into letting him stay at Cahill Lodge, a bed-and-breakfast place that Etta owned, for the summer so he could convince Roseanna to give her a second chance. That's what she'd been talking to her friend in Tulsa about on the cell phone when she dropped it and the car wound up nose down in a ditch.

The judge looked up. "Miss Greta Fields?"

"Yes, sir," she said. Eyes downcast. Shoulders slightly rounded. I'm sorry as the devil written all over her. She'd played this part before and it never failed.

He dropped his eyes back to the reports he'd been reading. "You are in a bit of trouble here, young lady. First of all, Mrs. Etta Cahill here has come to your rescue. She's made several calls on your behalf. Your father says he told you the last time you wrecked an expensive car that he wasn't bailing you out of trouble again and he's going to stand by his word, so he's not coming and not sending a lawyer. And he's shut down all the credit cards in your possession. Now, on to the more difficult news."

"I don't believe it. This old woman didn't call my dad. She and Roseanna are in cahoots to ruin my life."

The judge glared at Greta. "That's enough! Etta Cahill is not an old woman and you will show some respect in this room. She is your salvation, Miss Fields. She's the one who's trying to get you out of this mess you put yourself into. I've talked to your father this morning and informed him of the deal I'm going to offer you. He thought it was beyond fair. Now, according to these reports you were driving at a rate of ninety miles per hour in a fifty-five-mile zone. You dropped your cell phone and tried to retrieve it from the floor of your car when you lost control. That caused you to swerve over into the other lane and wind up in a ditch. By the way, your car has been towed out to the Cahill ranch but it's probably totaled. Your insurance has been cancelled according to what your father said this morning. Your driver's license is certainly revoked for the next four months."

Cold chills traipsed up Greta's backbone.

The judge went on. "When you lost control of your car, there was a pickup with a cattle trailer coming toward you. The driver, Kyle Parsons, jerked to the left and wound up with his rig in the opposite ditch. He lost a prize Angus bull he'd just bought and did not have time to list on his insurance, plus his trailer and truck have been damaged. The car behind him, driven by an eighty-five-year-old man, plowed into the back of the rig and is also totaled, and the one behind you hit the front of the rig. It's only by the mercy of God that no one was killed."

Greta felt as if an elephant had just parked on her chest. Simple breathing was a problem.

"There's no one to pay your fines so this is the only deal you are going to get. I figure at minimum wage it will take one hundred and twenty days of community service to work off what you owe. Or I'm going to let you sit in county jail for six months."

"You've got to be kidding. My brother will pay the fines for me," Greta whispered in a hoarse voice.

"That's not an option. It's A, county jail for six months, or B, community service. There is no C," the judge said.

"But . . ."

He pointed a finger at her. "No buts! There's barely a handful of people in the whole world who could talk me into coming into this office on a Sunday morning. You are lucky Etta is one of them. She's going to take you out to the Cahill Lodge where you will reside for the next four months. I think your time will be up the day after Thanksgiving. You will work for her helping around the lodge in the mornings. Are you trained for anything other than driving too fast and having too many accidents?"

"I have a degree in business management," she whispered.

"Good. Your skills can probably be used at the police department. Wilma has been pestering me to send her some help. Kyle here is going to pick you up just before noon each day and you'll work the same shift he does."

"Hey, wait a minute," a deep voice said from the corner. Kyle Parsons had been summoned to tell his side of the story about the wreck, not take the uppity Miss Fields to raise.

Greta jerked her head around to look into the dark eyes of the tall cop who'd been so brassy at her brother's wedding on Friday night and who'd yelled at her at the accident. His jaw worked in anger. If looks could kill she'd be a bag of bones on the cold floor. She remembered the way he'd been all condescending to her the previous evening, as if he were something other than a small-town redneck cop. And even worse, when he'd yelled at her for causing the wreck that killed his bull.

"I'm not going anywhere with him," Greta said.

Kyle bowed up to her. Lord Almighty, but he'd be crazy in four months. At least it was just a ride to and from the police department. "It's my bull that's dead and you'll do just what the judge says."

The judge shut the report and looked up at her. "Five days a week, from noon until eight o'clock in the police department doing whatever Kyle or Wilma says. If they need someone to clean files or type, you'll do it. If they need the toilets scrubbed, that's your job. And out at Etta's place you're going to work from eight in the morning until noon. So is it jail or are you going to leave with Etta? Those are your options, Miss Fields. You've got five minutes. My family is waiting for me to take them to church this morning."

Greta's skin crawled. She couldn't go back to jail. Six months inside that cubby hole would drive her insane. She might be spending life in prison with no hopes of parole if she had to put up with that cranky cop for four months because she'd kill him if he looked down on her every day. Not much of a choice.

The judge checked his watch. "One minute to go."

"I am very sorry I was rude to you, Mrs. Cahill. Thank you for your intervention on my behalf. I will try hard not to disappoint you. Your Honor, I would rather do four months of community service than spend six months in jail." Greta said in her best I'm-sorry-as-the-devil-please-forgive-me voice that always brought men to their knees. He'd change his mind, give her a severe lecture, and she'd be in Tulsa by lunchtime.

The judge stood up and adjusted his bright red tie. "Etta, you'll make sure she's not lazing around in the mornings? I want her to earn her keep at the lodge."

"There's plenty of work at the lodge and on the ranch. If I'm caught up, I'll send her to the barns with Jodie," Etta said.

Greta's heart fell all the way to her toes. Of all the Cahill women, she despised Jodie the most. A woman bull rider with an attitude bigger and meaner than a grizzly bear, she thought she was tougher than Superman and Indiana Jones all rolled into one. Jodie and Trey had clashed from day one, and it was only recently that they could stand to be in the same room together. Greta hadn't liked Jodie from the first time she'd met her five years before, and she'd made it a point to steer clear of Trey's apartment when Jodie came to visit her sister in Tulsa all those years. In her wildest imagination Greta couldn't see working in a smelly barn with Jodie. God, the jail cell began to look like a suite at the Hyatt Regency.

The judge paused at the door. "And one other thing. Officer Parsons here helps with a youth group at the Baptist church. That will be your weekend community service. If you'd been in jail, you wouldn't have gotten out on weekends, so it seems only fair you work those days in some capacity also. So Saturdays you'll go with

Kyle and help with the teenagers if he has something on the schedule. If not, you'll work eight hours at the lodge. Sunday morning you'll be in church and Sunday afternoons if there are youth-group activities, you'll help with those. If not, then your time belongs to Etta and she can give you a few hours off for good behavior if it's merited. If not, then you can work on Sunday too. Good day, Miss Fields."

"Yes, sir," Greta said meekly. They'd better keep all the guns behind lock and key at the Cahill ranch. She'd already begun a mental list with Kyle Parsons and Jodie Cahill at the top just in case homicide became legal in the next four months.

"This is Sunday. We don't have time to get you cleaned up for church so we'll get you settled in at the lodge. Kyle, what's going on this afternoon?" Etta asked.

The judge popped his head back around the corner. "Forgot one other little thing. Your cell phone was ruined in the wreck, but you are not to have another one. I catch you talking on a cell phone or driving a vehicle in the next four months, I'll add six months to your sentence and put you right back in jail. All six of your previous wrecks involved a cell phone. I'll be glad when the state of Oklahoma passes a law about those dangerous things. And you are definitely not to leave Murray County. You are here for four months, young lady. Is that understood?"

Greta nodded. Was there anything else these people wanted? Like her kidney or maybe her right arm? Her heart wasn't available. It was roasting in hell's furnace. Sassy as she'd always been, she knew to keep her mouth shut and swallow her pride. Four months and she'd shake the dust of Murray County, Oklahoma off her feet and never, ever look back. Until then, she'd simply drop off the face of the earth and cease to exist.

"We've planned a picnic in the Sulphur park after church, out on Travertine Island. Then the kids are going to swim awhile and maybe do some hiking. We'll be done at five so they can go home and get ready for evening services," Kyle said. "But . . ."

The judge shook his finger at her. "No buts. Her job begins today. Young lady, you will be ready at twelve o'clock. Kyle will pick you up."

Kyle Parsons fumed all during church services. At least Roseanna and Trey were on their honeymoon and not beside Roxie that morning. Not that he harbored any hidden feelings for Roseanna. No, ma'am, he did not. They'd dated for a few months five years ago but she'd burned her bridges with him the night she sang at the Arbuckle Ballroom in her sister's place. Defied him outright when he told her no woman of his was going to play and sing in a honky-tonk. Talk had it that it took a big man to tame a Cahill woman. He just hoped old Trey had his pants on real tight because it was possible even yet that Roseanna would be wearing them before the new wore off the honeymoon. But he was glad they weren't at church that morning because they might have talked that spitfire sister of Trey's to join them. The First Baptist Church of Sulphur, Oklahoma, wasn't big enough for Kyle Parsons and Greta Fields both.

Kyle was twenty-eight years old and had been on the police force for five of those years. Any one of the seedier people he'd dealt with would have been preferable to having to babysit Miss Rich-Hoity-Toity Greta Fields until Thanksgiving. He'd overheard her telling one fellow at the wedding reception that her parents had simply misspelled her name on the birth certificate. She was really supposed to be named Great, not Greta. Of course, it was supposed to be a big joke. But there was a note of sincerity in her voice when she told the tale.

The offering plate was passed. The benediction given. It wasn't until Roxie touched him on the shoulder that he realized he was still sitting and everyone else was leaving the church.

"You okay?" Roxie asked. She wore her signature ruffles and lots of them on a bright orange dress that morning. Her gloves and hat were white trimmed in orange and her spike heels, white leather with little orange bows at the toes.

"I'm ready to bite nails, Roxie," Kyle confessed. "You hear about Trey Fields' sister wrecking her car and causing a pileup yesterday?"

"Yes, I did. Me and Etta had us a long talk about things last night. I was willing to take that girl in but Etta said she was shirttail kin to the Cahill family so it was her responsibility. What's that got to do with you? I understand you'd be fired-up mad over your truck, and I heard you'd lost your bull, but at least she's at the Lodge, isn't she?"

"She's there in the mornings, but the judge put her in my care for the afternoons and weekends. She's to do community service at the police station through the week and help me with the youth group on weekends. I don't even like the uppity witch. She's twice as bad as Roseanna and it's a toss-up between her and Jodie," he said.

"That which does not kill us makes us stronger. They'll be calling you Samson by the time her sentence is done. She's a handful, that one is." Roxie smiled.

Greta changed from the jailhouse-issued clothing back into her muddy capri set she'd been wearing when she wrecked her brand-new Thunderbird convertible. The enormity of the wreck suddenly hit her nervous system like a class-five tornado headed for a tar paper shanty. Her hands trembled; her mouth felt as if it had been swabbed with cotton. If she'd had to spit or face a firing squad she'd have had to look the bullet in the eye. Her world had just fallen apart at the seams. Community service? Four months? It would be eternity plus three days.

She left the clothing in a heap on the floor and stepped on them on her way out of the cell. She walked out into the bright sunlight that late July Sunday morning to where Etta waited beside an old beat-up work truck.

Both the driver's window and the passenger's were rolled down, so evidently the air-conditioning, if the truck ever had any, no longer worked. Rust had eaten holes in the fenders and the tailgate was gone.

Greta shut her eyes and almost walked right back into the jail. She stiffened her spine and took a deep breath. Her father was not going to win this fight. She would show him that she was made of as much substance as her brother. She'd live through the four months without a whimper. That is, if she could ever get her insides to stop quivering.

"You ready?" Etta asked.

"I am and thank you again for getting me out of jail," Greta said.

"Family takes care of family. You ain't really kin but I can't leave you in a jail cell. Your car is settin' out behind the lodge. I reckon you've got clothes in it?"

"Only the dress I had on at the wedding reception and the outfit I wore down here plus this one." She sighed. No credit cards. One fancy dress. One ruined capri set and a pair of slacks and silk blouse.

"Well, I expect there's not that much difference in you and Rosy, and she left a closet full of work clothes at the lodge. Jeans. T-shirts and the like. What size shoes you wear?"

"Seven," Greta said.

"Good. That's my size and I've got extra sneakers and a pair or two of good broken-in work boots. You should be good for the rest of the summer." Etta turned right into the Chickasaw National Recreational Area, known to the locals simply as "the park."

"Thank you." Greta tried her best to be thankful even for the smallest gestures from the elderly lady, but it wasn't easy. She would have rather worn sackcloth and ashes than Roseanna's leftover clothing.

"You are quite welcome." Etta hung her left arm out the window and drove with her right one. "I could've brought the car. It's got air-conditioning, but it wasn't so hot this morning. Guess we're in for another scorcher. We need a good rain. Don't know why those folks in California fuss so about a rain. Lord, we'll take one any time we can get it, especially in July."

Greta studied the countryside. Rolling hills with tall trees, grass in need of water, wild flowers, and God only knew what kind of bugs and wild creatures were living in the whole mess. No shopping malls. No theaters. Nothing but nature and Greta hated nature.

Etta turned right down the lane to the lodge. "It's not what you are used to but you'll do fine, Greta. You're not some little weakling. You'll brace up and do what you have to do, and who knows, by the time you finish your time, you might even learn to like it."

"I don't think so. There isn't a miracle that big in the world and I don't believe in magic," Greta whispered.

Etta chuckled. She'd seen miracles and magic a lot bigger than the pretty young woman sitting beside her. She parked the truck in the backyard and led the way through the kitchen door into the lodge. "You spent the night here on Friday so you already know the general layout of the place. I'm not taking any guests this next week so Rosy can have a few days to get settled into her trailer and do some fall cleaning here at the lodge. She's still going to help out up here like she's been doing for a while. I'm glad to have your help so she won't have to work so hard. I'm about ready to retire and give this place to either Jodie or Rosy. Right now I'm just letting Rosy run it for me."

Greta stopped in the country kitchen, an enormous room with cabinets on three sides, an island in the center, and all the latest appliances. The refrigerator looked like it could house two or three elephants. The stove had two ovens and eight burners on the top. Bright red-and-white checkered curtains hung on the windows that overlooked the patio, where a built-in brick barbecue and a smoker were located. The walls were pristine white and sunlight flowed into the room through spotless windows.

Etta led the way past a breakfast nook with a table capable of seating ten people and chattered the whole way. "I'll show you up to your room. Built this place back fifty years ago. Same time as when Roxie bought her place on down the road. We'll go down there one night after you get home from work. Now that place is a piece of art. Roxie had it painted bright red with white trim. Sounds gawdawful but it's Roxie. She and Molly Brannon and I've been best friends these past fifty years. Molly died last year with a bout of cancer. She'd whipped it once, but it came back on her. Now there's just me and Roxie, and we've decided not to let the grass grow under our feet anymore. Every trip we take we think about Molly and all the times when we said all three of us would go, and then suddenly the time was gone for Molly. Here's the room you'll use. The bathroom is at the end of the hall. Two of them actually. One is set up for men folks. The other for the ladies."

Greta stepped through the door inside a bedroom. The walls were painted a soft yellow and pale yellow sheers covered the windows. Blessed cool air blew the curtains as it flowed from a vent in the floor. A quilt pieced of different shades of pastel gingham checks covered the fourposter queen-sized bed.

"This is nice," she said meekly. But where was Trey? He and Roseanna should be back from their overnight honeymoon and settled into that abominable trailer on the back side of the ranch by now. He should be checking on her even if he was angry with her, so where in the devil was he?

"Glad you like it. It's the room Rosy used the past few months. Figured I'd just put you here since there's clothing already in the closet. Just help yourself to whatever you need. I'll make it right with Rosy if she's got a problem with it. You might want a nice long bath to get all that mud out of your hair before Kyle comes for you. Oh, did you bring makeup?"

"I've got my travel bag out in the backseat of my car," Greta said lamely.

"Well, it's going to have to last you a spell so you might want to go easy on it, honey. Don't know why you'd even need makeup for a picnic in the park. You'd just sweat it all off anyway and you're a pretty young woman without it. Who knows what might happen between you and Kyle before the summer is over," Etta said with a twinkle in her hazel eyes.

"Nothing is going to happen between me and that redneck cop," Greta said quickly.

Etta laughed aloud. "I've heard that story before. You know where the towels are and where to put them when you're finished. Looks like it's already ten o'clock, and you need to be ready by noon. So don't be tarrying too long in the tub. I'll leave you to get settled in. Welcome to Cahill Lodge."

If Greta hadn't sat down in the rocking chair beside the window she would have fallen to the floor. Everything that had happened in the past thirty-six hours flowed over her like hot lava. She wrapped her arms around her body and hugged herself. How in the world had life gotten so complicated in such a short time? She was twenty-five years old, had finished her master's degree when she was twenty-three. She'd worked in and around the oil business but didn't actually have a title. There had always been something she could help with and her father paid her a handsome salary. At least until last spring when her whole world fell apart. Her brother was kidnapped, the company downsized, and she'd been living on her savings until she found a job she liked.

She made herself go to the closet and open the doors. Like Etta said—T-shirts and jeans. She moaned when she thought about underwear. She'd even be dependent on Roseanna for that. She slid a drawer out and found underpants and two bras. The bras would never, ever do. They were the right size around but at least two sizes too big. Until Christmas she'd have to make do with the one she was wearing and the black one in the car.

She went to the bathroom, shook a few bath salts sitting on the vanity into the claw-footed tub, and ran it full of warm water. A nice long bath and clean hair would make her feel better. She dropped her dirty outfit on the floor and kicked off a pair of cheap flip-flops the bailiff said she could keep. Her gorgeous red Prada heels were ruined . . . just like her life.

"I'm not a bad person. I know I've been spoiled, but I haven't done anything so horrid as to deserve this kind of punishment."

The water felt wonderful as she dunked her head into the depths to get her hair completely wet. When she came up for air it was as if she'd been baptized. She had a new resolve to see the whole sentence through with dignity. So what if she had to wear another woman's underpants. She'd live and the sun wouldn't stop coming up in the morning. Thank God Etta Cahill had been there when she called for her brother, and even more so for her intervention, or else Greta would be spending the day in a cell instead of up to her neck in a warm bath.

By the time she dried herself off and dressed in a pair of soft-worn jeans and a T-shirt with a picture of an eagle on the front, she was almost feeling normal. She padded down the stairs in her bare feet to ask Etta about a pair of sneakers and found Roxie at the kitchen table with Etta. No madam who'd ever hung a red light above her door could have held a light to Roxie. She wore brilliant orange and her red hair was ratted up in a do popular in the seventies.

"Hello, Greta. Kyle tells me you're going to help him with the youth group at the church. That'll be a good thing, I'm here to tell you. Those girls can use someone to teach them some class and you'll be just the ticket," Roxie said.

Etta motioned toward the island where salad makings waited. "We're having chef salads. Help yourself. You'll be eating hot dogs and hamburgers with the kids so it won't matter if lunch is light."

Greta filled a bowl and sat down. "Thank you for your vote of confidence, Roxie."

"Hey, I just call 'em like I see 'em. My granddaughter, Tally, spent a year in county lockup for hot checks a couple of years ago. Put her on the right track, it did. She's got a year finished in college now and a fine husband. Sometimes bad things aren't all bad and you might be surprised how this all works out. A lady holds her head up no matter if she's walkin' in tall cotton or deep manure. You remember that and you'll do all right, girl. Never know what this little spell in Murray County might bring." Roxie sipped the sweet tea beside her plate and went on. "Kyle Parsons can be more than a little self-righteous. Told Rosy no woman of his was going to be singing at the Arbuckle Ballroom a few years ago. Thought he could call the shots with a Cahill woman. Don't you be lettin' him lead you around by the nose, girl. He'll do it if you let him so you go into this thing with both your dukes up and ready to fight for your rights. It's all right for a man to wear the pants in a marriage, but they don't have to be ugly about it."

"I couldn't care less about his ego. I speak my mind, so Mr. Parsons might not want me to help with the youth very long if he's a male chauvinist."

"It'll take a special woman to tame Kyle," Roxie said.

"I'm not that woman. I intend to pay for my mistakes and get out of this place. Trey seems to be happy, and I don't mean any disrespect to either of you, but I'm not a country woman. I'd die without the lights and action of the big city."

She'd barely finished eating when someone knocked on the back door.

"Come on in," Etta yelled.

Greta finished her last bite, put her plate and glass in the sink. "Etta, you mentioned that I could borrow a pair of shoes?" She deliberately ignored the rude policeman. He might look as sexy as a movie star in those tight jeans and wraparound sunglasses, but she wasn't interested.

Etta motioned toward a pair of red Keds beside the door. "Right here. We'll rustle you up some other ones later."

"Thank you," Greta said. "So, Mr. Parsons, I suppose my sentence begins right now."

He stepped aside and held the door for her.

She let herself into his big black double-cab pickup truck, grateful that the darkly tinted windows were rolled up, giving testimony to the fact that there was air-conditioning. She fastened the seat belt and waited.

He slid into the driver's seat and clicked his seat belt. "Let's get something straight right here at the beginning. I don't like you. I don't like this arrangement. You are a spoiled brat and could've killed several people with your reckless driving. Your driving record is horrible and if they never let you drive again it would be doing the world a favor."

"Are you finished?" she asked.

He nodded.

"Then let's get something straight right here at the beginning. I don't like you either. The only thing bigger than your ego is your belt buckle. The number of fingers you have on your right hand probably exceeds your IQ. I don't give a damn what you think of my driving, and it's not up to you to revoke my license forever so your opinion doesn't matter. I have to work with you for the next few months. I can make it pleasant or I can make it hell. You choose."

He started up the truck and backed out, kicking up

dust behind the wheels. "Oh, honey, you've met your match." He drew out the word *honey* as if it were something nasty rather than an endearment.

"Darlin', you couldn't straighten out Roseanna Cahill and she's a baby kitten compared to me," she retorted.

Chapter Two

Greta pushed strands of long jet-black hair away from her sweaty face. If God would have wanted her to be outside in the heat, fighting mosquitoes and slapping at gnats, he wouldn't have let ultrasmart people invent air-conditioned condos, automobiles, and shopping malls. Etta had been right when she advised her not to waste makeup. She would have sweated it off in the first five minutes. Already, after barely half an hour in the cruel summer elements, her neck was wet and she kept wiping at her forehead and upper lip. A steady stream poured down the inside of her one good white bra. Salty sweat stung her eyes and she wondered how in the world anyone could enjoy this kind of Sunday afternoon outing. Wouldn't it have been much better to take the kids to McDonald's for burgers and then to an air-conditioned movie?

Her nostrils flared at the smell of nature all around her. And the noise! Above the hullabaloo of ten pubescent teenagers a steady racket of bugs kept up a hum not totally unlike white noise on the television set. She'd prefer the perfume counter in Neiman Marcus any day of the week instead.

Kyle had introduced her to the horde of kids whose names she'd never remember: five pimply faced boys who all looked alike with baggy shorts hanging low on their hips and loose fitting tank tops showing off scrawny arms and shoulders, and an equal number of girls in faded T-shirts covering up their bathing suits.

"Greta, bring me a paper plate. Hot dogs are ready," Kyle said.

"I'll get it," one of the girls said. "Hey, Jim, get away from those chips. We haven't even said grace yet."

"I'm hungry," Jim protested.

She swatted him on the arm. "You won't starve."

"Stop hitting on me, Kelsey." Jim flirted.

Kelsey blushed. "I wouldn't hit on you except to knock you stone-cold, Jim Landry, and you know it."

Greta almost smiled. That Kelsey might be a smart kid after all. At least she was putting one of the male species in his place. Kelsey with a bad haircut, gorgeous blue eyes, and braces. Not Chelsey, but Kelsey. She'd remember that name and make an effort to remember one name each time she was forced into sponsoring one of these backwoods affairs.

Kyle piled the hot dogs high on the plate and Kelsey carried them gently to the table. If one could call it a table. In his I'm-so-much-smarter-than-a-city-girl tone, Kyle had explained about the table as he cooked. It was built in 1934 by the CCC and had withstood natural storms as well as thousands of picnics through the past seventy-plus years. It was a long rectangular slab of rock with benches on three sides. The strange thing looked more like a sacrificial altar than a place to put grilled hot dogs and hamburgers. Maybe it had been there long before the CCC came along and they just took credit for it. It sure looked like something one of those Old Testament priests would have offered a ram or six turtledoves upon. She bet if she checked the bottom of the slab there'd be burned places where they laid the wood. Or did they pile it up on the top and then scorch the sacrifice?

She unfocused her eyes and imagined Kyle in white robes all laid out and ready to be offered up to the gods; a smile on his face and a halo hovering around waiting to land on his head until he'd officially died. That vision disappeared quickly when she remembered how he'd screamed and yelled about stupid rich women and their cell phones at the accident site. No angel-in-waiting would have used the language he did, or the tone either. Great God Almighty, she'd simply dropped her cell phone. If she'd known the pompous cop she'd met at her brother's wedding would be driving his prize bull down the road, she never would have even made that phone call. Drat the bad luck anyway.

The next vision she conjured up was one of him during his college days when he and "the good ol' boys" brought a portable CD player and a suitcase of beer to the island on Saturday nights. Maybe that's what turned him into a self-righteous youth director: too many Sunday-morning hangovers.

Jim mumbled a quick grace and twenty elbows vied for space to make their hot dogs and/or hamburgers. Innocence knew no social lines and hunger pushed away manners every time. Greta smiled in spite of the heat and noisy bugs.

"Ah, the ice queen smileth," Kyle said.

The woman was lovely, at least on the outside. Long black hair, straight as a board and cut to feather around her face. Even pulled back in a ponytail, it beckoned him to run his fingers through the silkiness just to see if it was real. Thick eyelashes and perfectly arched brows to frame eyes so dark they looked ebony. Flawless skin with a pert nose and full mouth, a delicate chin that would just fit into a man's hand, and a slender neck that begged to be kissed. Exterior beauty. Interior spoiled so rotten the garbage man wouldn't carry her off for the promise of wealth beyond comprehension.

"Not at you." The smile vanished when she looked at him.

Blasted man anyway. Acting all pompous at the wedding reception. Raising his voice about a stupid bull when he strutted across the highway to rant and rave about a bull rather than asking if she was hurt. Not caring that she'd just busted the heel off her shoe or that she had mud in her hair. Or even that her car was totaled and she might be hurt herself. No such luck. That big hunk of hamburger on the hoof was more important than a woman in distress.

Oh, Kyle was a piece of eye candy for sure. Tall, well built, sandy brown hair cut too close for her taste, but then what did a small-town cop know about hairstyles? Hazel eyes that could cause a nun's panty hose to crawl down around her ankles. A chiseled face that would look very, very good in subdued candlelight. Not that she'd ever see him in dim lighting—or that she'd want to.

"I'd grab my running shoes and light a shuck for the outback of Australia if I thought you were smiling at me, lady," he said.

"Hey, hey, you two better grab some food before Tim catches his second wind," Kelsey yelled over her shoulder at Kyle and Greta.

Greta brushed the back of her jeans and picked up a paper plate. She couldn't remember the last time she'd eaten anywhere where china wasn't used. She could never remember fanning flies away from food before she ate it. She opened a bun and began to follow Kelsey's example. Grilled hot dog, mustard, chili straight from the can, which had been heated on the grill, onions, cheese, and a little sweet relish. She pulled a fistful of barbecued potato chips from a bag and put them on the plate, balanced it all with one hand and fished a cold Dr Pepper from the cooler and carried it all to the sacrificial lamb table.

Kelsey moved inward and motioned to her. "Come sit by me. So tell me, what's going on with you and Kyle? Isn't he the dreamiest thing in the whole world? If he wasn't so old, I'd flirt with him."

Greta swallowed quickly to keep from spitting food across the whole tiny island. "Nothing is going on with me and Kyle."

"Well, rats. There's a dollar I just lost. I bet Tim that you were his new girlfriend. Okay, then, don't you have the sweetest dreams about him? Maybe if you're nice to him he will be your boyfriend."

"If I dreamed about that man it would be nightmares, not sweet dreams," Greta said.

Kelsey giggled. "If you're not his girlfriend, then what are you doing here?"

Greta wondered for the hundredth time if she'd made the right choice when she'd opted to go with Etta Cahill. "Staying out of jail."

Kelsey finished the last bite of her chili dog. "You're so funny. I'm going to like you. Hey, Tim, you ready to go swimming?"

"Not me. This is just my first hot dog. I don't stop at less than half a dozen. Hey, Kyle, you going to eat or not?" Tim said.

Kyle held up a set of oversized tongs. "I'm eating and cooking at the same time."

There was only room for one more person at that table and it was right next to Greta Fields. Kyle would rather have been paired up with a hungry rattlesnake.

Before Greta could finish her lunch, all ten kids had devoured theirs and were in a race to see who could get back across the footbridge to the place where Kyle had parked the church van.

"Why can't they get wet here? The water all looks equally disgusting," she said.

Kyle gritted his teeth.

"Are you going to answer me?" she asked.

So she wanted him to talk, did she?

"Travertine Creek gets its main water supply from Antelope and Buffalo Springs. It's called Travertine Creek because the water that comes from Antelope and Buffalo Springs contains dissolved lime from underground deposits. Aboveground the limestone is redeposited as a porous substance known as travertine.

"Years ago, the CCC was commissioned to construct several dams along Travertine Creek. One of the most popular ones is called the Little Niagara waterfall and maintains an average temperature of sixty-five degrees year round, which makes for a nice cool swim for the kids in water deep enough to actually swim in instead of wade. There are seventy-five natural rock falls and six man-made dams on Travertine Creek. And that's all in only two and a half miles.

"When this was just Indian Territory, the Indians used to gather the nuts and store them for winter. They were not a wasteful people. They used the husks from the walnuts and pulverized them, then stirred them into the pools of water. For some reason it stunned the fish so they could be caught, then the Indians would dry them for the cold weather when food was scarce.

"The trees overlooking the water where you are sitting, those with peeling, paper-thin whitish bark and broad leaves are sycamores. You will also notice red cedars and mixed prairie grasses, such as the little bluestem, the Indian grass, and broadleaf dangle grass. Other plants in the area are prickly pear cactus and yucca. Anything else you would like to know about the park?"

Greta didn't miss an ounce of the sarcasm in his voice. "Thank you for the insightful information, Mr. Tour Guide. I'll remember to refrain from asking you anything else. We might be here through eternity if I asked why the mosquitoes are as big as Texas buzzards."

"Longer than that. If you like the sound of my voice, I could educate you on the mosquito's origins and how—"

"Oh, spare me. Are my duties here over? Am I allowed out of your sight, Mr. Jailor?"

He made one more sweep of the area, picked up a napkin that had blown back under the table and the plastic top from a water bottle, and put them into the trash. "Make up your mind. Am I tour guide or jailor? You can carry the sack and I'll take the cooler."

She hated following him. The symbolism was disgusting, but she had no idea which way to go. She could hear the kids yelling, the water flowing over the rocks, the crickets and the frogs on both sides of the bridge. Even though the island was scarcely bigger than a good-sized ballroom, she didn't want to be left alone to find her own way back to the van.

He set the cooler with soda pop and water on one of the tables in the shaded area beside the place where the kids were playing. "And now your duties are over. Put your sack right there. They may want a snack or something to drink when they finish swimming. Water makes them hungry. The Nature Center is that rock building you can see over that way." He pointed off to the right. "Or you can claim a table and watch the people."

"What are you going to do? And tell me in one word. I don't want a two-hour lecture."

"Watch," he said.

"Then I'm going to the Nature Center. And one other thing. What is the CCC? Please . . . in as little words as possible. I don't care about the bark on the sycamore trees," she said.

She just thought she had the upper hand with her snide remarks, Kyle thought as he sucked in a lungful of air and began, "CCC stands for Civilian Conservation Corps. It was a work relief program for young men from unemployed families back in 1933. It was part of President Roosevelt's New Deal legislation and was designed to combat poverty caused by the depression. Of course, you wouldn't know anything about that since your family probably never knew a day's poverty."

She shot him the meanest look she could manage.

"About two hundred men made up a camp and they stayed for six months and were paid to do outdoor construction work. The castle over at Turner Falls in Davis was built by the CCC camps too. After the depression, the CCC lost importance. That's about as few words as I can use. Now if you want personal experience stories then have a seat and I'll entertain you for a while."

"Oh, sure, like you were around seventy years ago," she smarted off.

"No, but my grandpa was and he was glad to have a job in the CCC, and he's told me stories," Kyle answered lazily, refusing to let her see how she riled him. There was no way he'd ever let her have that much power.

"Talking too much must be an inherited gene." She walked away but the deep chuckle behind her grated on her nerves.

The first thing that caught her attention when she reached the Nature Center was a pay phone hanging in an alcove. Her heart skipped a beat and her eyes glistened. The judge said she couldn't have a cell phone. He dang sure didn't say a word about using a land line or a pay phone. She dug down into her jean pockets and came up with a dollar bill. When she'd popped the trunk on her demolished car and taken her things into the lodge, she'd found a few loose dollars and some change in the bottom of the makeup kit. With renewed purpose she opened the door into the dimly lit interior of the Center, and asked the man behind the small gift counter to exchange her dollar for quarters.

Leaving the cool interior somewhat reluctantly, she plugged a coin into the phone and made a collect call to her best friend, Monica, who accepted it readily. "Monica, I'm in big trouble and need your help."

"Why are you calling me and reversing the charges? Where is your cell phone? And what's this I hear about you having a wreck when you were talking to Miriam?"

Greta was so thankful to hear a familiar voice that she didn't even mind the heat. "I did have a wreck. They think my car is totaled. I dropped the phone and was trying to retrieve it when I lost control."

"So when are you coming home?"

"Four months. I'm on community work for four months. Father wouldn't bail me out of this one. Monica, come down here and pay the fines so I can come home. I'll pay you back, I promise," Greta begged.

"Not me, darlin'. If Vance Fields didn't bail you out, then I'll be damned if I will. Daddy would cut off all my credit cards and put me to work full time. You know he and Vance are poker buddies and play golf together every Saturday morning. You are askin' me to do too much."

"But you're my best friend," Greta said.

"Yes, I am. When you get home, call me and we'll go shopping and have lunch."

"Will you at least drive down here and see me? Bring me some clothes from my apartment and there's a credit card in my file cabinet in my name only. I'll pay the bills on it, just bring it to me and I'll use it to pay my fines. It's in the second drawer, under the heading Personal . . ."

"No thank you. I'm not getting in the middle of your family battles, Greta. Not when it might jeopardize my world. Have fun down there in the boonies. When you get back to civilization, call me. Lunch is on you since you owe me for this call. Bye now," Monica said.

Greta held the phone for a full two minutes after the dial tone returned and the mechanical operator kept repeating that if she wanted to make a call to first hang up and then dial again. Even though she wanted to jerk it from the wall and throw it in the creek, she squared her sagging shoulders and went back inside the coolness of the Center. She spotted a bench toward the back of the room and sunk into it. Not even Monica would come to her rescue, and they'd been friends since they were infants. Their mothers were friends. Their fathers were old frat brothers. She was alone in the wilderness, quite literally.

She focused through eyes misty with unshed tears at the turkey and deer in a floral setting right in front of her. Once upon a time they'd both ran wild through the world and now some taxidermist had forever set them in Sulphur, Oklahoma, for people to ooh and aah over. Greta was that deer. Once she'd been free. Now she was a prisoner in Sulphur, Oklahoma. Four months was eternity and beyond. What a mess she'd gotten herself into this time.

With a heavy heart she meandered further into the quiet room. Stuffed animals were everywhere. An armadillo, horned lizard, collared lizard, and a coachwhip snake, all in one glassed area. Stuff Kyle Parsons and he'd fit right in there with them. "And here's the living replica of a Sulphur cop. Mean as a snake. Hard-shelled as an armadillo. Has a lizard heart and mean eyes just like one," she whispered. "Well, you won't get the best of me, Kyle. I'll show you I can take everything you can dish out. Just be careful you can do the same."

"Who are you talkin' to?" a little girl asked at her side.

"Myself, I guess," Greta answered, unaware that anyone was near.

"I'm sorry. She doesn't know a stranger." The child's father took her by the hand and moved away.

"Quite all right," Greta said, but they were already gone. No one wanted to hear what she had to say that day.

Several displays were arranged down the center of the room. One caught Greta's eye as she headed for the door. It was called the Chickasaw Nation Connections Display and had a handmade quilt above it. Kyle could probably tell her some long-winded tale about how his grandmother pricked her finger on the sixth day of creation when that quilt was made. So her grandmother hadn't made quilts and her grandfather hadn't worked for the CCC. That didn't make her any less of a person.

She wasn't a bad person just because she'd been born into a wealthy family. She briskly left the cool building to go back out into the wilds. She'd show the lot of them . . . and then she'd go home and have it out with her father.

Over to her right, the creek ran swiftly. Five stepping stones down to the water looked like they'd been tossed there by nature, but those CCC men probably placed them carefully. Did they play in the cool water after a hard day of setting stones perfectly so people could use them like the steps into a real swimming pool? She noticed a small fish taking its time swimming around a little island of natural grass and flowers. The whole island was so small she would have had a hard time sitting on it without getting wet. Were those flowers some of the ones Kyle had mentioned? Something called dangle grass?

Sun rays beat down upon her head and arms like heat from an oven as she walked on toward the swimming place. A red-and-white painted fire plug looked as out of place in the natural setting as she felt. A few marshmallow-looking clouds floated around in the pale blue sky, but not enough to blot out the stinging heat from the sun. Crickets and other wild animals kept up their songs as if they were in paradise. How could anything sing in weather like this?

When she arrived back at the place where the kids were still swimming, she chose a table well away from Kyle and watched the people. Big. Small. In between. Mother Nature didn't give a hoot about size. She offered her services to everyone. Come on to Sulphur to the park and have a good time in the cool water. Bring your bologna sandwiches and hot dogs and use my wooden tables and benches. Take happy memories home with you. Greta sighed. The memories she'd take home in a few months wouldn't be happy, and she'd forget them as soon as she shook the dust of Sulphur from her feet.

She watched a little Hispanic girl in a bright yellow bikini with red daisies and her little brother in one of those floating swimsuits. The girl had a toy fishing rod and had hopes, no doubt, of catching a little fish with it. The boy carried around a green net, dipping it in the creek and bringing up nothing more than a few wisps of algae and grass. Both seemed happy just to be at the water's edge with their toys.

The boys and girls she and Kyle were responsible for played some kind of water game. Girls against boys. She hoped the girls won but didn't watch them very long. Her attention went back to the children. Someday she wanted a daughter and a son. A family. But they'd never play in a place like this. She'd have a swimming teacher come to the house, to her private pool in the backyard to give them lessons.

"Time's up," Kyle yelled from the bench where he'd been reading a book. "Gotta go or you'll never have time to get ready for church tonight."

Amid groans and moans and one more toss of the ball, they all came out and wrapped up in towels.

Kelsey sat on the top of Greta's table and put her feet

on the bench. "You should have at least took off your shoes and put your feet in the water. It felt so good."

People ate off these tables, sometimes without the benefit of even a paper cloth, Greta thought. Feet, hind ends, big old green flies, and who knew what else found its way to the tabletops, and then little boys and girls like the ones swimming laid their sandwiches down on the tables. She shuddered at the idea.

"No thank you. I'll let you have all the fun," Greta said.

Kelsey hopped down and took off toward the van. "Maybe someday before the weather is too cold, you and Kyle will take a dip with us."

"Not in your wildest nightmares," Greta mumbled.

"Whose nightmares. You been dreaming about me?" Kyle was close enough behind her that she could see the five o'clock shadow on his face.

She stood up and dusted off the seat of her jeans. "If I did it would be a nightmare, for sure."

It took thirty minutes to deliver each and every kid right up to their door. Kelsey lived in a small brick house. Jim, in a white frame that needed paint. Molly, in a big old rambling two-story not far from the Oklahoma School for the Deaf. Andy, in a trailer out in the middle of a pasture.

Neither she nor Kyle said a word during the process or on the way back to the lodge. He parked out front and she opened the door.

"You don't have to get out. I know how to let myself in," she said.

"I'll get you at the door and walk you to it when I return you. It's part of my job, woman," he said.

Her temper flared. "Don't you ever call me *woman*. I'm not backwoods white trash. I have a name and don't you forget it." She shook her finger at him.

Kyle followed her up the steps onto the porch. "Sure thing . . . *woman*."

She drew back her hand to slap him. "I mean it."

He reached out and grabbed it in midair. "I wouldn't do that. It would be assaulting an officer and I reckon you could draw another hundred and twenty for that."

Every bone in her body tingled with something she attributed to anger.

Every nerve in his body reverberated with something he figured was pure rage.

Etta broke the scenario from the doorway. "Got a problem out here?"

"No, it's nothing," Greta said.

"Well, then come on inside. I left you a note on the table. Don't forget to set your alarm. Your workday begins at seven-thirty tomorrow morning. This is a slow week. You and Roseanna will be cleaning in the mornings. Next week, you'll be getting up at five-thirty to help with breakfast. I'm off to Roxie's for lemonade on the back porch. The ledger is beside the phone in the foyer. If anyone calls check it before you make reservations. Have a good evening. See you tomorrow about noon Kyle." She waved from the steps and left a puff of dust behind the truck.

"Tomorrow at noon . . . *woman.*" Kyle nodded toward Greta.

"I'll be ready . . . *man,*" she said.

She went up to her room and threw herself across the bed. Two days ago she was Greta Fields, one of the most eligible young women in Tulsa. In less than forty-eight hours she was reduced to being called *woman* and working as a maid.

"But looking on the bright side," she said aloud, "day one is finished. Only one hundred and nineteen to go. And like Grandmother Fields says, 'A pity party can only last fifteen minutes and your time is up. Besides, who wants to go to a silly old pity party anyway. There's no one else there because no one wants to attend something that boring. There's no cookies and tea and sure not a drop of chocolate because who'd waste such good things on a sad party. So get up and get on with life.' It's a whole lot easier said than done, Grandmother. I'm not having a pity party anyway. I'm having a reality check, and it's scarier than anything I've ever done."

Chapter Three

Roseanna sat at the kitchen table, the morning newspaper in front of her. "Good morning, Greta. Coffee is in the pot."

Etta Cahill had riled her granddaughter, Roseanna, by letting Trey move into the lodge back in the spring, but that was nothing compared to the way Roseanna felt about coming home from her honeymoon to find Greta living there. Greta, who'd always looked down her snooty nose at Roseanna, who'd caused her no end of grief—not only living at the lodge but working with her at least four hours every day. The tension in the room couldn't have been cut with a good sharp butcher knife.

Greta filled a cup and pulled out a chair. She might as well get the ordeal over and done. It couldn't be any worse than the afternoon she'd spent with Kyle the day before.

"Understand you are hired for four hours a day to pay for your room and board," Roseanna said.

Greta sipped the coffee. "I guess so."

"Seven-thirty to eleven-thirty and then Kyle picks you up for community service until eight every evening." Thank goodness Roseanna would be back in her own home with her husband, Trey, by then. Four hours was going to tax her patience to the breaking point.

Greta looked across the table and talked to the newspaper in front of Roseanna. "That's right, and if you're going to gloat then do it all right now. Having to work with Kyle is going to be depressing enough without listening to you every morning too. Thank goodness you threw him out the door all those years ago or you'd be stuck with him right now. Him and all his male attitude and ego. But then if you'd kept him, I wouldn't be here today, would I?"

The newspaper fell and Roseanna glared at her sister-in-law. "I'm not here to gloat or ride roughshod over you. I'm a hired hand just like you are. I don't agree with what Granny Etta did, but she has her reasons. I didn't like it one bit when she allowed Trey to move in here, but it sure worked out. So don't go getting uppity with me. Granny Etta says you will work four hours a day for room and board and that's getting off cheap since the lodge room alone rents for a lot more than what you'll make. On the mornings when you have to get up early to help with breakfast you will be paid minimum wage for those hours. So if you've got a mind to work, she's willing to pay for anything more than four hours. If you want to work on Saturdays or Sunday afternoons after church when Kyle isn't keeping you busy, that's the possibility of more money. It's up to you, lady. There's a work record in the top drawer of the foyer table. Keep track of your hours and she pays once a week. Granny trusts you to be fair. You've got about fifteen minutes if you want breakfast. I'd suggest you eat since we are going to be working hard and you'll get almighty hungry before lunch if you don't eat. There are leftover eggs and sausage on the stove top. Trey made extra in case you were hungry."

Greta never ate before midmorning and then it was a latte and biscotti from Starbucks or a smoothie when she got to work. She surely didn't eat fat-filled eggs and sausage, but with the idea of four hours of housework ahead she filled a plate. "Where is Trey and when did he learn to cook? I suppose he's really getting a laugh about all this?"

"Trey is a more complex person than you ever gave him credit for being. He had to go to a faculty meeting early this morning. They're gearing up for the new school year. So we cooked and ate earlier than usual. And he's not real happy about you being around either, but we'll both live through it, I'm sure. He'll be around to see you when he has time and cools off."

"How was the honeymoon?" Greta asked between bites. The food was very good. Maybe she'd been missing out on breakfast all these years.

"Fine."

"That's all? Just fine? Is the bloom already fading?" Greta asked.

"Greta, I have to work with you, and that wasn't exactly what I wanted to hear when I came home from a wonderful weekend with my husband. But I don't have to endure your biting remarks. If you can't say something decent to me then keep your mouth shut. We can work together without speaking. It might not be pleasant, but it can be done. Your choice."

A smile tickled the corners of Greta's mouth. In moments it was a full-fledged grin. A small giggle quickly changed into a belly laugh that took both of them by surprise. Never in her life had Greta laughed so hard or so long. Finally, she picked up an oversized white napkin and wiped her eyes. She stuck her hand out over the plate of eggs and sausage and looked Roseanna in the eye. "Truce?"

Roseanna slowly reached across to shake the woman's hand. "What came over you?"

"Your choice," Greta said and was off on another set of giggles that brought on the hiccups.

"What's so funny about that?"

"I wish you could have seen the look on Kyle's face yesterday. It was lightning and thunder and rage all rolled into one. He thought he was going to be some he-man Neanderthal and jerk me around by the hair. He said his piece. I said mine and let him know it was his choice whether this would be a decent four months or hell. I could make it either one. Then I told him you were a kitten compared to me and he couldn't tame you," Greta said between hiccups.

It was Roseanna's turn to laugh, and in the midst of two women giggling over coffee and eggs, the faintest threads of a friendship began.

"I'm finished. Let's go to work. I'm either getting up at the crack of dawn tomorrow or working a couple of hours after I get in tonight. I've never worked for minimum wage in my life but right now it sounds pretty darn good. Is there a clothing store in Sulphur or even in Murray County? I'd like to buy a few pair of my own underpants and a bra or two," Greta said.

"Got to admit, I figured you'd choose different. Why Murray County? You can shop in Ardmore or Ada or run up to Norman or down to Gainesville, Texas, for clothing, but I don't think there is a place to buy . . . oh, there's Wal-Mart."

"Can't leave the area according to the judge. I'm doomed to Murray County for four months, but at least there is an end and I get to go home when it's over. Never bought a thing other than toilet paper and paper towels from Wal-Mart, but when I get my first paycheck I'm going to beg someone to take me there. And Roseanna, I'm choosing to call it a truce with you and maybe even with Trey if he stays out of my way most of the time. He could have paid my bail and gotten me out of this mess. Four months in this place looks like forever from this end, even if you and I do bury the hatchet. I'll be out of here so fast when this sentence is served it'll make your head spin. One thing is for absolute sure, I don't ever intend to call a truce or be friends with Kyle. That's asking way too much of my limited supply of patience. Now, let's get at this housework thing you were talking about. I've never done that kind of work so you may have to do some teaching along the way."

Roseanna raised an eyebrow.

Greta crammed the rest of a biscuit in her mouth and looked at the clock. "No driver's license. No insurance. No credit cards. No cell phone. Life as I knew it is dead, but I'm still breathing and the self-pity party is over. Seven-thirty. I'm ready."

Roseanna could scarcely believe this was the same woman who'd done nothing but despise her. Five years ago Greta had pitched a hissy fit when Rosy married Colin Vance Fields III, or Trey to all his family and friends. Almost a year ago they'd divorced and Greta was all smiles. In the spring, Greta had driven to Sulphur with the news that Trey had been kidnapped and the ransom was a million dollars. Would Roseanna, an expert tracker, rescue him? Rosy had done that, and in the process, lost her heart again to her ex-husband.

Just three days before, right after the marriage ceremony, Greta had said, "You both have my sincere sympathy. I can't think of a single reason why this wedding happened." Surely Greta hadn't changed so much in a mere three days.

"You're wondering about things. It's written all over your face. You Cahills can't hide a thing. If you're happy, it's right there in your eyes. If you're mad, same thing. I still think you and my brother are mismatched but hey, it's his life. If he thinks a double-wide trailer on the backside of a farm is living then that's his prerogative. Personally, I think he lost his mind when he was chained to that tree up there in those mountains. I haven't changed, Roseanna, I'm just making the best of a very bad situation."

Rosy smiled. "Life can throw you some big rocks, Greta. Let's get on with scrubbing and waxing the dining room floor. It'll take all morning."

Greta rolled her brown eyes. Day two wasn't going to be any better than day one.

"Dratted woman. Greta the Great. That's who she thinks she is, but she'll never convince me of it. Wish I'd never stopped and talked to Samuel after I bought the bull. If I'd have come on home instead of jawing around with him for ten minutes, I'd have been past that stretch of highway where she dropped her blasted old cell phone." Kyle talked to his Catahoula cow dog on the front porch of his trailer. He'd already done the morning chores. Feeding the cattle. Mucking out the horse barn. Harvesting the tomatoes and okra. The rest of the garden had dried up weeks ago.

Amos Smith stepped around the end of the trailer. "Think that dog can answer you?"

"No, and I'm not talking to you today either," Kyle said.

"What's your problem?"

"Greta Fields."

Amos sat his tackle box on the bottom step and leaned against the redwood porch railing. "She's too much for you to handle?"

"There ain't a woman alive who's too much for me to handle."

"That's not what I heard a few years back. Heard Roseanna Cahill got the best of you. Thought maybe when she divorced the big hotshot oil man and came home you might make another try for her, but then you let him step right in and here she is married again. Since it was your property that got ruined in the wreck, I figured you might like a second chance at redeeming yourself. I can always put Greta doing community work from nine to five on Wallace's shift. He could be in charge of bringing her to and from work. Wouldn't want you to put up a *No Trespassing* sign on my favorite catfish pond in the county just because you're all in a huff about a pretty lady's work schedule."

"I told you I can handle her. What are you doing out fishing on a Monday anyway?"

"Kids are at school. Wife is off shopping and the court docket is free today. How'd yesterday go?"

"Slow. Four months might not be enough to get the

job done. She's a handful, all right. It'll take a long time to tame that one. Don't know if it can even be done."

"If it's not, I'm sure you'll figure out some way to extend the time. Think the fish are biting today?"

"If they're not, you'll figure out a way to make them, I'm sure," Kyle smarted off to Judge Amos Smith.

Amos chuckled down deep in his chest, picked up the tackle box, and headed toward the farm pond. The warm summer breeze carried the sweet pure strands of the judge whistling "Statue of a Fool" back to Kyle.

Greta took a quick shower, washed her hair and dressed in the best jeans and plain T-shirt she found in the closet. She'd barely finished a ham and cheese sandwich and bowl of tomato soup when Kyle knocked on the front door. He stood to one side and held the door open. She stepped out into the blistering hot heat. Monica would never believe Greta was being escorted to work by an officer in full uniform—complete with a gun on his hip and a radio on his shoulder. At least he was driving his big black pickup truck instead of the official police car with all the lights and whistles.

Kyle was a fine specimen of the male species with muscles in all the right places filling out a gray and navy uniform. She might have been attracted to him in another life if he didn't have that irritable attitude. But it wasn't another life and although she'd always liked uniforms, she'd never give him a moment of her time. Not with his women-are-property viewpoint. The judge laid down the rule that she had to ride to and from her community service job with him, but he hadn't said a word about having to talk to the man.

Kyle thought back to the night of the wedding. The first time he'd looked across the corral and seen Greta, he'd thought he'd laid eyes upon an angel dropped down from heaven. She'd worn a red dress that hugged every curve of her body. Trey had teased him about not letting Greta drink Murray County water since it was rumored that anyone who drank it always wanted to return for more. Kyle had made the comment that he sure didn't want Greta coming back, and yet here she was. If she wasn't such a spoiled brat of a woman he might have truly been interested even at the reception, but it was evident from the first time she opened her mouth to talk down to him that she thought she was on the same level as the Queen of Sheba.

Neither of them said a word the whole way to the police station. At twelve o'clock on the dot he punched his time card into the clock. "Follow me." He motioned to Greta.

Before he took a step, a woman opened a door. She had short gray hair that was either naturally curly or freshly permed into one of those Kizzy Jane styles. Bright blue eyes set deeply in a bed of wrinkles and looked huge through thick eyeglasses edged in rhinestones.

She started at Greta's toes and worked her way up to her hair. "This my new help?"

"This is Greta Fields. She'll be here from noon to

eight, Monday through Friday. Judge says when you leave at five every day to give her enough to keep her busy until my shift is over," Kyle said.

"You got any training of any kind other than speeding, talking on the cell phone, and killing bulls?" Wilma asked.

"I have a degree in business management and I've worked in my father's oil company for several years," Greta said. She'd only been intimidated a few times in her life, but this was one of them.

"Know a blessed thing about computers? Get on out of here, Kyle. You just have to bring her to me, not stick around and listen to every word we say. Go to work. Write tickets. Keep the citizens law-abiding." Wilma pointed toward the door.

"Gladly!" He disappeared out the door.

"Yes, ma'am. I do know a thing or two about computers," Greta said.

"Then come on back here and I'll keep you busy for years instead of months. We're trying to get all the old files put into the computers. I type slower than a snail and I hate to do that data input crap." Wilma led her into a room no bigger than a good-sized walk-in closet. A desk occupied one wall and boxes upon boxes surrounded it.

"I've been working on this box. It's from the fifties. Case concerns a black man shot to death by a couple of white boys. During the time when the schools were being integrated. Doesn't matter what they're about, though. We just need them put into the computer so the information can be retrieved by other law agencies as well as us. Think you can do that and then forget all about it when you go home?"

Greta sat down at the desk, adjusted the desk chair, and began to type where Wilma left off. "Yes, ma'am."

"Well, halle-damn-lulah." Wilma grinned. "At that rate, you might get through most of these boxes by Thanksgiving. Thank you, darlin', for havin' a heavy foot and a cell phone. I don't even care about Kyle's dead prize bull if you'll keep up that speed. I may kiss Judge Amos right on the mouth for giving you to me. You keep going and I'll be back about three to get you for a fifteen-minute break. Can I get you anything?"

"Yes, ma'am, I'll take a hot, single-shot, tall, nonfat caramel latte with double whipped cream from Star-bucks."

Wilma threw back her head and cackled. "So would I, honey. How about a bottled water? It's cold. Or a cup of coffee straight from a ten-cup Mr. Coffee?"

"Water is fine."

"After Thanksgiving I'll go with you to Ardmore and we'll get us one of them Starbucks things, and if you get all this work done, I'll even pay for the thing," Wilma said.

"It's a date." Greta kept typing and didn't even look up when Wilma slipped back inside and set the water beside her. This wasn't going to be as bad as her night-mares the night before. She'd dreamed that she was out-side in the sweltering heat painting the entire courthouse with a one-inch brush. Although the shoe box-sized room couldn't be classified as an office, at least it was cool. The boxes upon boxes of files surrounding her were more than a little daunting, but she didn't have to finish them by Thanksgiving. She merely had to work at it eight hours a day.

When Wilma knocked on the door frame at three o'clock, Greta could scarcely believe she'd been working that long.

"Let's take a break. Want a doughnut? Got some in my office, and coffee too, even if it ain't one of those things with a mile-long name in French," Wilma said.

"I'd love a doughnut and coffee. I don't care what the coffee is as long as it's black and strong," Greta said.

Wilma opened a box of doughnuts when they reached the front office. "So tell me what you think of Kyle Parsons. Have a seat right there. I'm so tired of that chair I could cry. I sure don't want to spend my break time sitting in it. Plain old glazed or chocolate?"

Greta wiggled her neck, working the kinks out. "Chocolate. I've earned it."

Wilma laid two chocolate-covered doughnuts on napkins and handed one to Greta. "Yep, I think we might be friends."

Greta looked at the screen on the monitor. "What are you doing here?"

"Damned old payroll. Takes me forever. I could get the job done faster back in the days when I kept books by hand and wrote out the checks the same way."

Greta bit into the doughnut. "Mmmm. I could help you with that. We used a different program at the oil company. It's a lot faster and simpler than this one."

Wilma pulled a folding chair near. "Show me."

"Let me see. Yes, I thought this computer would come equipped with this program already installed. Okay, here it is. Here's your spreadsheet. Fill in the name, the amount of gross, and just a minute . . ." She typed in Murray County and Oklahoma in the right spaces. "There. Now it'll figure out the taxes, social security, Medicare, and standard deductions for you. Then when you need to make your monthly reports for . . ." She was about to say the board of directors, but in a city government, it wouldn't be that.

"The City Council meeting," Wilma finished the sentence for her. "When I have to make a monthly report, all I do is tell it to print, right? Here you go." She handed her the payroll sheets. "You enter all this in the new program and I'll go ahead and do it the old way too. We'll keep double records for two months until I get on to it. But first, you're going to have your break. Finish your doughnuts and drink that coffee before it gets cold, and tell me what you think of Kyle."

"I think he's an overbearing, egotistical, self-righteous macho man who thinks women are possessions or animals and it's his duty to God to tame or kill every woman that comes in his sight. Good doughnuts, even if they aren't Krispy Kremes."

The wrinkles around Wilma's mouth quivered but

she didn't smile. "Other words, you think he's a fine-looking man in that uniform and he makes your little heart go pitter-patter, but you ain't about to admit it until you see if you can rope him in."

"I'm not interested in roping him in. I just want to do my sentence and go back to Tulsa where my life is."

"Uh-huh," Wilma nodded. "Don't say that too loud. The Good Lord has a sense of humor and sometimes he likes to throw monkey wrenches in your plans."

"Amen."

"What kind of man are you lookin' for?"

"What makes you think I'm looking?" Greta asked.

"It's the way of things. Some of us get married when we're barely dry behind the ears. I was fifteen and that was fifty years ago this Christmas. Some of us wait until we're forty. Might as well fess up and tell me what kind of feller you'd be willing to settle down with. What kind of man do you dream about?"

"Rich. Good-looking. Already established. Who can offer me the lifestyle I'm accustomed to living. A traveler would be nice so we could go to Rome or Paris on a whim. That answer your question?"

Wilma shook her head. "Hell, no!"

Greta jerked her head up. "Why?"

"I didn't ask you what you want from the man. I asked you what kind of man is in your dreams. That means, what does he have to do to make you feel like a queen, not how much he can give you. Shut your eyes, Greta."

"Why?" Greta asked but did what she was told.

"That's what you do when you go looking for a husband. You don't look at what he looks like or what he's got. You look at the man on the inside. Is he strong or weak? Weak means you could run over him, and no woman wants a weakling. Is he strong enough to make you feel safe and secure in his arms without taking who you are away from you? Are you going to have to fight with him occasionally? Does he make you feel all tingly and alive? Does he make your nerves stand on end just by touching your arm in a café?"

"That's pretty hard to answer. But I'll keep it all in mind when I decide to go looking for a husband." She opened her eyes at the same time Kyle opened the door and led a man inside the office.

"Drunk driving," he said to Wilma. "I'm taking Clement here back to a cell to sober up. His car is parked out by the sale barn. Said he didn't want to call his wife; that she wouldn't come get him anyway."

Wilma reached even as she spoke. "Got the report?"

Kyle handed it over. "Right here. What's she doing in here? I thought she was supposed to be typing for you."

"Don't you be worrying none about Greta. She's on a fifteen-minute break, and if you or Amos don't like it then you can come see me. She's just saved me a ton of hours during her break anyway, not that it's a bit of your business. She's mine once you get her here so just do your job and leave us alone."

Kyle shook his head.

Greta bit the inside of her lip. It was worth every kink in her neck to see Kyle put in his place. Wilma must have squatted in a field years and years ago and they built the police station around her for her to have that much power. Judge Amos scared the bejesus out of Greta and Wilma was daring him to say a word. Greta wondered if she could be coerced to move to Tulsa and work for Fields Enterprises?

Wilma glanced at the clock behind Greta. "Break time is over. Back to work. Take another doughnut with you. I'll be leaving at five and you'll be here alone until eight. Oh, the dispatcher will be in there." She pointed toward a window. "But basically you'll be on the honor system. I don't think I've got a thing to worry about with you, girl. But just in case you get a wild hair to do something crazy, remember, it can be a long four months or a short one."

Greta grinned and almost broke into more giggles. "My choice?"

"That's right. I'll see you at noon tomorrow."

"Thank you for the doughnuts and coffee," Greta said.

"Quite welcome. Thank you for helping me with that payroll. Tomorrow when you get here you can work the first little while on helping me transpose everything into that program. Lord, I'll be glad to retire come the first of the year. Some little young thing fresh out of college can do this job with all this newfangled equipment."

"It's not so difficult, Wilma, once you get on to it," Greta said.

"Trouble is, I don't want to get on to it. I want to go home and forget all about it."

"What are you going to do when you retire?"

"I'm going to sit down in that white rocking chair on my porch and after the first six months, I plan on starting to rock back and forth. I'm going to throw the alarm clock out in the yard and mow around it and sleep all the way up to seven o'clock every morning. The rest of the time I'm going to do nothing," she said.

"Sounds exciting." Greta went back to her own desk and almost had the file finished when Kyle poked his head in the door and told her it was eight o'clock.

"Give me five more minutes and I'll have this done," she said.

"Shut it down. I've already clocked out and I'm going home now. You can go with me or walk."

She clicked the right buttons to save her work and turned off the computer. "You are insufferable."

"And you are spoiled."

She fumed all the way to the lodge where he insisted on walking her to the door.

"Job done. See you at noon tomorrow," he said.

She glared at him and went inside without a word.

Jodie peeked around the kitchen door. "Well, well, don't the world turn round?"

The fairly nice day just got worse. Roseanna's sister, Jodie, and Greta had sized each other up the first time they'd met, and both had come up short in the other's eyes. To Jodie, Greta was nothing but an overbearing fashion queen. To Greta, Jodie barely qualified as a woman with her cowboy boots and hats.

"What are you doing here?" Greta asked through clenched teeth.

"I came in from the hay field for a bowl of Granny's soup. I'd ask you the same thing but I already got the story from Roseanna. Hungry?"

"Starving and too dang mad to eat," Greta said.

"Soup's hot and on the stove. Help yourself. I'm just finishing my first bowl and headed for the second," Jodie said.

She looked like she'd been rolling in dust all day. Her hands and face were clean but her jeans, shirt, and even her rugged old cowboy boots were filthy.

Greta dipped up a bowl of vegetable soup and picked up a piece of cornbread. Jodie crumbled the bread into her soup so Greta followed her example.

"You look like warmed over sin. How did you get so dirty?" Greta asked.

"I'm in the hay field. I'll be there until midnight or after, then I've got to clean the horse barns. It's going to be a long, long old night, but that's what happens this time of year. 'Course a city girl like you wouldn't know a thing about working. Your day ends at five o'clock," Jodie said.

"Etta said she'd pay me minimum wage for any work

I do past the four hours a day for my room and board. You got anything I can do? I'm so mad I could commit homicide. Maybe I can work off the anger," Greta said.

Jodie's eyes twinkled. "You serious?"

"As a full-fledged cardiac arrest. Either I'm going to murder Kyle Parsons or else . . ." She let the sentence hang.

"Or else explode. Men folks have a way of making us feel like that. Are you sure you want to work? Can't do much in the hay field. Not nowadays. Back when we made little square bales, you could have loaded them on the truck, but we've gone to the big five-foot-round bales. But that's not the only work on the farm. You can muck out the horse barns if you want to." Jodie sipped sweet iced tea to keep from giggling. The visual of the almighty Greta Fields trying to clean up horse manure was almost enough to set her off into a case of giggles.

"I'll do it," Greta said.

Jodie spewed tea halfway across the table. "Girl, you wouldn't be worth a teaspoon of salt in the horse barns. You'd do so much damage that I'd spend the rest of the night cleaning up after you. I was joking with you. You don't know jack squat about farm work."

"I can learn and don't you talk to me like that. You're as insufferable as Kyle. Both of you think you are one step up from God."

Jodie actually grinned. "Kyle just thinks he is. I'm more convinced. You ever been around a horse barn?"

"Once or twice."

"Can you handle a horse enough to lead it out of a stall?"

Greta nodded. Jodie didn't need to know that her grandfather had a ranch in Texas and grew some of the finest thoroughbreds in the whole state. Granted, she'd never cleaned a stall in her life, but she knew how.

"Okay. If you don't create a disaster, you can make some money tonight. If you do make a big mess I have to clean up, you owe me fifty dollars, payable at the end of the month. Still want to work?"

"You got a deal. And if I don't create a disaster, as you say, then you have to take me to Wal-Mart on Friday after I get home from the police station."

Jodie's eyes widened. "What for?"

"No questions. You just have to do it."

"Deal." Jodie nodded. "But I've got to sing at the Arbuckle Ballroom until midnight on Friday so it'll have to be after that or else on Saturday morning."

"After midnight is fine. Wal-Mart does stay open twenty-four hours down in this part of the state too, doesn't it? I've got to go to Falls Creek with Kyle on Saturday morning at nine o'clock. The kids are having a retreat up there. Yippee, yeah!" She said sarcastically. "Anyway, I want to go to Wal-Mart and at least buy some of my own underpants."

"Kyle's not so bad. Granny Etta says it takes a professional woman to henpeck a man and him never know he's been henpecked. It'll take an ultraprofessional woman to henpeck old Kyle. He has to be macho to show the world that he's all mean and tough. Someone will come along one of these days who'll tame him," Jodie said.

"I'm not sure there's a woman with breath in her lungs who'd want him bad enough to work that hard," Greta answered.

Chapter Four

Kyle's jaws worked in anger as he drove west from Sulphur toward Davis. One week and Greta had him ready to hang up his badge and pistol. No one ever got ahead of Wilma and in only five days, she treated Greta like an equal. Amos Smith could usually see right through a scam, and evidently, Greta had him eating out of her hand because he'd given Kyle orders to take her to the Arbuckle Ballroom after-hours that night instead of taking her home.

"How'd you do it?" he finally asked.

Greta shook her thick black hair loose from a clamp and let it fall down her back. "Do what?"

"Don't play the innocent little lamb with me. I know you're just using all my friends to get what you want. Bat those eyes and use that soft voice and . . ."

She glared at him. "Are you accusing me of using people?"

"Exactly."

"Why would I do that?"

"To get your way. What else? Work hard and get on Wilma's good side. Then she puts in a word to the judge so you can go out partying tonight. You are a sly one," Kyle said between gritted teeth.

She looked straight ahead. "I don't have to explain anything to you."

She wouldn't let sour apples ruin the lovely evening or the brilliant orange, bright yellow, and pink sunset. She'd earned every moment of this evening. Not that she'd have chosen an evening in a country dance hall listening to country music, but she'd always wondered what the Arbuckle Ballroom looked like, and tonight she'd find out. Five years ago, when Fields Enterprises was a lot more lucrative, Trey had trouble with the company limo and wound up at the Ballroom. He met Roseanna there and a month later they eloped.

Besides all that she wanted to see if Jodie could sing as well as everyone said. Did she hop up there on the stage, grab a microphone, and sing in her dirty old jeans and broken-down boots?

Kyle parked in the middle of the crowded parking lot. "Here we are. All I've got to say is that you'd better be ready tomorrow morning. If you aren't, then Judge Smith will hear about it."

"So you aren't above tattling?"

"It's not tattling. It's reporting on the parolee."

"I'll be ready," she said. "Are you coming inside with me?"

"No, I am not. I encourage my youth group to stay out of such places. What kind of example would it set if I went in there?"

"Ever been in such a den of iniquity?" She teased.

"Many times but for business—to drag some belligerent drunk into jail."

She stepped out into the hot summer night breezes and headed toward the front door. "Okay, then. I'll see you in the morning bright and early."

He put the truck in reverse and had his foot on the gas pedal when he saw three big burly men swaggering toward Greta. He braked and waited. Maybe they'd walk on past her without a word. No such luck. They started whooping and hollering loud enough he could hear them over the buzz of the air conditioner. He turned the key and opened the door about the time the largest one grabbed her arm and spun her around.

"Don't you dare touch me." Greta pushed away from him only to back into one of the other ruffians.

"Okay, Will," Kyle said quietly from right behind the man. "Either get on about your business or I'm taking you to jail."

Willard Kemp held up both hands in innocence. "For what?"

"Assault. Resisting arrest. Public drunkenness. Anything else I can figure out. Leave the lady alone or spend the night in jail and give the county your next week's paycheck in fines," Kyle said.

"Whew!" Will said with drunken bravado. "Pardon me, ma'am. I thought you were my wife. She's supposed to join me here tonight."

One of the other men guffawed. "Sandy is blond-haired. You really are drunk if you think this filly is your wife."

Kyle took Greta's elbow and escorted her toward the front door. "Let's go."

"I could have handled that by myself," she protested.

"Probably, but it's my job."

"You are off the clock, Kyle Parsons. That knight-in-shining armor syndrome is embedded so deep in you that you can't get rid of it even when you don't like the damsel in distress." She didn't like the way her elbow fit so well into his big hand or the effect his touch had on her.

"I don't have any such syndrome and you are most certainly not a damsel in distress. I have no doubt you could take care of yourself. You could cut them to ribbons with that sharp tongue of yours. I didn't want to be called back to work and have to fill out two hours worth of forms because you hurt one of those big old boys," he said sarcastically.

A man who should have been playing pro football waited inside the door. "Hi, Kyle. Someone call the police?"

"No, I'm just escorting this lady inside," Kyle answered.

"You're comin' in for pleasure, not business?"

Greta bit her lip to keep from giggling.

"That's right. Only it's not pleasure. It's protecting my parolee, here."

"Parolee? What were you in for?" the man asked.

"Cell phone. Speeding. Six-time offender at wrecking a car," she said sweetly.

The man chuckled. "Kyle, you know the drill. You'll have to check your hardware right here if you're coming in for pleasure. No guns, cuffs, or any such thing. Now, if anyone calls the station and I tell them you're here anyway and in uniform, then I can give them back for you to do your job. Otherwise, you can pick them up when you leave."

Kyle handed over his equipment and led Greta to an empty table in a back corner. She sat down and took stock of the place. Jodie and her band were on the stage playing a whiny country song. People hung on one another and swayed back and forth on a crowded floor. Greta had to admit, Jodie cleaned up well. She wore skin-tight creased jeans and an ecru lacy blouse with a ruffle down the front and around the bottom. Her hair was tucked up under an off-white cowboy hat. Even though Greta wasn't overly fond of country music, she had been exposed to it at her grandparents' ranch in Texas. Grandmother, born in Boston, had tried to reform Grandfather, and she'd done a superb job in most areas, but she'd never gotten past his love for country music.

"Hey, how about a little bit of Terry Clark. Gear it up

for 'A Little Gasoline.' " Jodie breathed into the microphone before the drummer hit a couple of licks and the fiddle player dragged the bow across the strings.

She sang about packing it up and heading west and just needing a road and a little gasoline. Greta could sure relate to that, only what her heart needed wasn't a road headed west, but one going north, back to life and civilization. She could use a road and a little gasoline and she'd be doing just what Jodie said about pushing herself and the old machine. Pretty soon she was tapping her foot to the music.

A cowboy appeared at the table and smiled down at her. "Care to dance?"

Kyle answered for her. "Sorry, she's just here to wait for a ride."

The man nodded and disappeared into the crowd.

"I don't need you to talk for me," Greta protested. "Maybe I do want to dance. Why don't you go on home? I'm twenty-five years old. I'm not near a cell phone or car keys. You've done your duty. Now go away."

"I'll stay awhile." Truth was he loved to hear Jodie sing. Loved country music. Greta gave him the perfect excuse for sitting along the wall and listening.

Greta leaned to the side and yelled into his ear. "Then you *will* dance with me. I'm going to dance while I'm here and I don't care who it's with. So don't be running off any more offers."

The song ended with heavy applause from everyone on the floor.

"I've got a request. Guess we woke up the crowd to Terry Clark. Someone has requested 'To Tell You Everything.' So here goes," Jodie said.

Greta raised an eyebrow at Kyle and stood up. Jodie crooned about souls who didn't reach out and something about telling a man everything—every secret, every regret, every mistake. The day had never dawned that Greta wanted to look into a man's eyes and want to tell him everything. She really, really couldn't imagine telling Kyle anything much less everything, but by dang, he would dance with her. She'd been good all week long and she wouldn't ask him to share a beer with her. Just a few simple dances in this place that was the furthest thing from a ballroom she'd ever seen.

"You can't dance?" Greta asked. "So be it. I'll find someone already on the floor."

He was on his feet in a split second and held out his hand. The tingle glued him to the floor, but he ignored it. He stopped at the edge of the floor, pulled her close, and began a fast two-step that practically took her breath away. "I can dance," he said gruffly.

"I believe you can," she agreed.

The dance ended too quickly and Jodie handed the microphone to the violin player. "This is for you older folks out there. Grab your partner and let's do a little George Jones and slow this night down a little bit while Jodie takes a break."

Kyle headed back toward the table. He'd danced

with the woman. Now they could sit down and wait until the band stopped playing. Then he'd turn her over to Jodie and his day would be finished. Before he could take two steps she grabbed his arm and literally spun him around.

She wrapped her arms around his neck and melted into his arms. "I'm not finished dancing."

The way she felt scared the pure devil out of her but she'd overcome it if she had to dance with this small-town cop until dawn. She chalked it up to a week of boredom in Murray County. Granted, she'd stayed busy, but every waking minute had to do with work, not play. This was the first time in a whole week that she'd had fun, and that was counting last Friday night when she'd danced a few times in the corral with a few country bumpkins at the wedding reception as fun. It hadn't really been a good night and neither was this one. But it was the best she'd had and she'd make the best of it.

The violin player did a fine job of George Jones' voice. He sang an old song entitled "Walk Through This World with Me." Her grandfather loved that song and often asked for it so he could dance with her grandmother. Bless her heart, she'd adapted to his countrified ways in the more than fifty years they'd been married. Grandfather would like Kyle. Greta drew her thoughts up short. Grandfather would never meet Kyle. When she left Murray County, she'd never look back, so there wouldn't be a reason for her grandfather to be around Kyle.

The singer asked her to walk through this world with him and to go where he goes. He wanted her to share all his dreams and said he'd look for her for a long, long time. That was the very story of her grandparents and she hoped someday she'd have such a wonderful relationship. One where she would walk through the world with someone important enough to share all her dreams.

Kyle kept perfect time. He could have stepped on her toes a few times or missed a beat. When the song ended, he didn't move but went right into the next one. He'd teach the wench to pressure him into dancing. He'd keep her on the floor until she wore the soles off her shoes and her legs ached so badly she couldn't sleep. Then he'd insist on a two- or three-mile hike tomorrow while they were at the summer retreat for his youth group. She might win a few battles, but the outcome of the whole war would be in his favor.

The singer sang "She's My Rock," and Kyle thought about his mother. His father often sang this song to her. Off-key. Out of tune. And his mother loved it. Kyle would never settle for less than someone who'd be the sunshine of his days, just like his mother was to his father.

They danced through three more George Jones tunes, then the singer turned the microphone back over to Jodie, who kicked up the pace with Gretchen Wilson's "Redneck Woman."

Kyle surprised her when he threw an arm over her

shoulder and joined a dozen or more line dancers. Greta about lost him when he executed a triple step backwards, locked his left foot behind his right one, and moved perfectly with the other people. By the time the song ended, she was breathing heavy.

A lady fluttered her eyelashes at him. "Good dancing, Officer. Come on over to our table. We'll brew you up a little something to whet your whistle."

"Thanks, but I don't drink."

"On or off duty?" She ran her fingertips down the curve of his jaw and lightly touched the dimple in his chin.

Greta wanted to jerk the woman's arm off and beat her to death with the bloody stump, but she held her peace. The woman was twenty years older than Kyle, and if he wanted to keep company with her the rest of the evening, then he could just jump on it. There were plenty of people in the ballroom to keep her dancing until Jodie stopped singing.

"I don't drink, period."

She leaned in closer, almost kissing him. "Then what are you doing out here, Officer?"

"I'm dancing. Love to dance. Love country music. But I do not drink. Excuse me." He led Greta out to the middle of the floor.

"If you love dancing and music then why don't you come out here other than for business?" she asked when Jodie began a slow song.

"I have to be an example to the youth of the church. I can dance and listen to the music without drinking. Could they handle the pressure?"

"I don't think thirteen-year-old kids are going to have that problem. Not a one of those kids could get in here even with a fake ID," she said.

He didn't answer.

At eleven-thirty, Jodie sang one last tune and Kyle led Greta to the bandstand. "I'm putting her in your care now. I understand you are to take her home."

"That's the deal. She tell you what she did for this night?"

"No. What?"

"Nothing," Greta said. "Thank you for the dances. Like I said, you could have left at any time, but I did enjoy the night. You are an excellent country dancer."

"I bet those words about gagged you to death," he said.

"You will never know how much," she told him.

"See you around, Jodie," Kyle said and headed toward the door.

Jodie unplugged microphones and helped the band members break down the equipment. "Want to tell me what happened here tonight?"

"Nothing happened. I wanted to dance and he ran off the first person who asked me, so I told him that he had a choice. He could dance with me or I'd dance with whoever came around."

"Didn't look all that innocent to me from where I was standing," Jodie said.

"Trust me. It was. Can I help with this job? I want to go to Wal-Mart and then get some sleep. He says he's arriving early tomorrow morning and if I'm not ready, he'll report me to the judge."

Jodie threw back her head and laughed.

Greta couldn't imagine what was so danged funny.

Chapter Five

Greta stretched out in the bottom of a three-bunk bay. The girls' side of the cabin was capable of sleeping twenty kids, so the girls had all chosen lower bunks and were already fast asleep. No wonder. They'd played hard all day. Volleyball. Hiking. Swimming. They'd eaten just as heartily and laughed just as readily.

It hadn't been easy keeping up with them after the previous late night, but she wouldn't have complained if it had killed her graveyard dead. Not for one second would she have given Kyle the pleasure of knowing she was worn to a frazzle. Of course, he didn't have any idea she'd been working four hours a night after she'd put in eight hours at the police department. But at least after her late-night run to Wal-Mart the night before, she wore her own underpants and a new bra, and she'd paid for them with the money she'd earned. She'd even parted with a few dollars for a bathing suit on sale for less than half price.

Greta shut her eyes and tried to will herself to sleep. Tomorrow morning started at seven with breakfast, which she and Kyle had to cook. After that there would be morning devotionals and getting all ten kids loaded into the van and the short trip back to church. She hoped she wouldn't fall asleep during the sermon. Maybe she'd sit between Jodie and Roseanna. She'd be afraid to fall asleep for fear one of them would accidentally murder her.

She'd be ready for a long, long nap after Sunday lunch, but she wouldn't get it. She'd already promised Jodie that she'd work. If she wanted a paycheck next Friday, she had to work for it.

She replayed the telephone call that morning from her parents. Her father had talked first. He was still angry after a whole week and declared he would never pay her automobile insurance again. Also, that she'd been removed from the payroll at the company and would have to find a job when her community service was finished. She'd gritted her teeth and told him she was a grown woman and could take care of herself.

Her mother was a little softer. She offered to go to Greta's apartment and pack whatever she needed and have it sent to Sulphur. She even asked if she needed money to buy necessities. Greta refused both. That's when her mother lowered the final boom. The lease on her apartment, which the company had paid for, was up for renewal on September 1. What did she want done with her furniture and belongings?

"Put them in storage," Greta had said.

"Okay. I've checked into a climate-controlled place. Looks like it will be about a hundred dollars a month. I'll see that it's all packed and taken there and pay your first month's rent. After that it's your bill. Your father says you are on your own so that's stretching what I'm supposed to do."

"Send me the papers and I'll take care of it," Greta told her.

She kept replaying the conversation, thinking of things she could have said, things she could have done differently. Finally, she eased out of bed and padded barefoot across the dining room and out to the porch. She sat down on the steps and leaned against the railing. She had been spoiled but no more than Trey— maybe not as much. She hadn't ever taken the company jet to Houston or used the company limo to impress a date. A hundred dollars a month for her storage would mean working almost seventeen hours for Etta or Jodie. She'd work twice that much to avoid asking her father for one penny after the way he'd ranted.

And why in the devil hadn't Trey come to her rescue? Granted he was busy with his new job, but it wouldn't have cost him more than a few minutes to stop by and make sure she had necessities at her disposal. When he did make an effort to see her, she vowed she would give him a solid piece of her mind. And if he didn't come around soon, she'd walk to the back forty and deliver that piece of her mind in person.

She sighed. She was a reverse Cinderella. From riches to rags in the space of a moment. Born with a silver spoon in her mouth and designer clothing on her back. Now she was lucky to have one of Roseanna's faded nightshirts and Etta's cast-off sneakers.

Kyle sat down beside her, carefully keeping a foot of space between them. "Can't sleep? I thought you'd be snoring by now."

She drew the knit nightshirt down over her drawn-up knees. "What are you doing out here?"

"Jim and Andy both snore. Nice clear night," he commented.

Good Lord, was Kyle being nice?

"What are you thinking about?" he asked.

"You wouldn't be interested in my thoughts," she said. "Tell me about you, Kyle. You from around here or are you an import like Trey?" Anything to keep him from asking questions she didn't want to answer. He'd get a real charge out of her backwards Cinderella story.

He stretched out his long, muscular legs and planted his feet on the bottom step, leaned back on his elbows, and gave it a few minutes. Did he want Greta to know anything about his life? She could ask Wilma or anyone else in town and they'd tell her all the uninteresting details of Kyle Parsons. There were a few secrets the small town of Sulphur didn't know, but not many.

"You want it in one word or you want the long version?" he asked.

"I can't sleep, so give the whole story and bore me. If I fall asleep, just throw a blanket over me and leave me alone until morning," she said.

Did he detect a sense of humor in the wealthy princess? Would wonders never cease?

"Okay, just remember, you asked for it. My ancestry has been traced back to the Kickapoo Indian chiefs who brought their sick folk to the springs back even before Coronado ever arrived in the Oklahoma area. That would be about five hundred years ago."

"You have Indian blood?"

"Sure do and so do you, so no snide remarks about it."

"How did you know?"

"Honey, you've got all the features. Thick black hair, straight as a board. Dark eyes. High cheekbones. What tribe?"

"Don't be calling me honey. It's either an endearment that you have no right to or a sarcastic remark that I don't want to hear. And it's Chickasaw."

"It wasn't an endearment. Anyway, this area was known as the Field of Eden. My great-great-grandfather came here with the military way back when. Of course, he wasn't aware that my mother's people had already laid claim to part of the land years before. He fell in love with the area and swore he'd come back. It took a while, but he did. Meanwhile, the curing powers of the mineral springs began to spread and brought people to be healed. Anyway, by the time the first store was established in about 1885 and the town, named Sulphur Springs, got its first post office in 1895, Grandpa had a house and was farming. He married a Kickapoo squaw and his people disowned him. White men didn't marry Indians in those days."

"You're telling me a tall tale," she said.

"Truth. Cross my heart," he declared.

"My grandfather and his siblings were children in 1907 when statehood came around. Grandpa was one of the men who fought the businessmen who wanted to fence off the springs, sell lots, and close the water from the public. Lord knows, he believed that water could cure everything from ingrown toenails to the plague."

"So long story is that your roots go very deep in this area."

"That's the long story. What about you? Where's your Indian? You got deep roots somewhere?"

"No. Grandfather's grandmother had some Chickasaw. Never did have a roll number, but she had Indian blood. Back then folks weren't so eager to step up and claim a roll number. It was a disgrace. His father founded Fields Enterprises back in 1916 when the oil boom hit Oklahoma. I'm not even sure why he went to Boston in the mid-fifties, but he met Grandmother there and they married. They had one son who carried on the business. Father and Mother had Trey and that's the only child they planned, then oops, I was born. End of story. We lived in California. Then we moved to Tulsa about the time I finished high school so I got my college education there. No roots. Who needs them?"

"I do. They give me stability. I went away to college right out of high school. Couldn't wait to get out of this small hick town. Four years later I couldn't wait to get back. Had a few offers for jobs in the big city making more money, but I wanted to come home. Ever heard that song Rascal Flatts does about broken roads?"

"Sure, I've heard it. It was popular a couple of years ago," she said.

"Well, listen to it next time it comes on the radio. The singer blesses the broken road that brought him home. That's me. I couldn't wait to get away, and that broken road circled around and brought me right back home."

Greta yawned.

"Bored yet?"

She stretched her legs out, moved down a step, and propped her bare feet on the step with his. "Not enough. Got any more of those long stories?"

He chuckled. "I think I've told you everything from Genesis to Revelation."

"Ever wonder what would have happened if your great-great-grandfather had gone to Boston and married a rich lady?"

"Then I reckon I'd have a whole different accent and I doubt if I'd wear cowboy boots or be a policeman in Sulphur, Oklahoma. Do you believe in fate?"

"No, I believe we make our own way in the world. Fate has nothing to do with anything. It's cause and effect. We create a problem—we pay for it. We do something good—we get paid for it."

"Kind of like driving too fast with a cell phone in your ear?" he asked.

The nice friendly mood flew away on the evening breeze.

"Why did you bring that up?" she snapped.

"Cause and effect. You said it. I didn't." He smarted right back.

"That's right. I caused it. I'll pay the price. Then I'm out of this place. I don't want roots to grow in Sulphur, Oklahoma. My brother thinks he's happy here. I'm not so sure he's not living in a bubble. When it breaks, he'll get restless and come on back to the city where he belongs."

"So your broken roads are going to lead you back to the big city?"

"Yes, sir. So fast it's going to take a lot of effort for anyone to ever remember I was ever here. The day after Thanksgiving I'm either going north to Tulsa or south to Dallas. I'd suffocate in this place if I had to live here forever. As long as there is an end in sight, I can endure it."

"Are you sure you're tough enough to even endure it until the day after Thanksgiving?" he asked.

"I have no choice, but yes, I'm that tough. I'm going inside now. Thanks for the stories."

Why had this woman gotten under his skin? It wasn't fair. From the time he looked across the corral two weeks ago she'd been pestering his dreams. He'd be glad when she did light a shuck back to her big-city ways and he could forget all about her.

She tiptoed across the center room that incorporated the kitchen, dining room, and lounge in one area. The boys' bedroom was on one side and the girls' on the other: lots of room in between so there could be no fraternizing of the sexes during a retreat. She smiled. All they had to do was meet on the front porch and no one would know if they'd talked away half the night. She eased the girls' bedroom door open and shut it just as carefully, made a trip through the bathroom, and found her bunk in the dark without stubbing her toe or falling over a piece of furniture. She congratulated herself on the victory and shut her eyes.

In moments, she fell asleep only to dream of Kyle Parsons. He wore Indian buckskins and a feather in his long, dark hair. Muscles rippled down his chest and abdomen, and a strip of rawhide was tied around his huge biceps. He rode bareback on a big black horse into the yard where her parents lived in Tulsa. Her mother's Porsche was parked in the driveway beside the company limo. Kyle didn't react to the expensive cars or house. He pointed at her and told her father he'd come to ask for her hand in marriage. Vance put her on the black horse behind Kyle with only the clothes on her back. She awoke in a sweat at dawn, sat up too quickly, and bumped her head on the upper bunk. She stumbled across the floor and into the bathroom, where she washed her face in cold water and looked at her reflection in the mirror to make sure it was just a dream.

"What's wrong? You sick?" Kelsey asked.

Her presence startled Greta, who hadn't heard anything but the pounding of her own heart. "No, just had a horrid nightmare. What are you doing up this early?"

"I'm a morning person. Get up at five every morning. I love the quietness of the morning time. I like the sunrise. I know it's crazy. All my friends sleep until noon on Saturdays and barely get up in time for church on Sundays. They also don't eat breakfast, but I do. Eggs, bacon, sausage, biscuits. All of it. Momma says I've always been this way. What'd you dream about?"

Greta changed the subject. "It doesn't matter. Let's go watch the sunrise."

Torture wouldn't drag the details of that vivid dream from her mouth.

Chapter Six

"What are you trying to prove? That you can kill yourself in four months? You're not used to hard work. Long hours, yes, but not work like this." Trey propped his elbows on the gate to the stall beside the one where Greta shoveled wet hay and manure into a wheelbarrow.

Greta turned slowly. "Ah, so the favored child decides to make an appearance after nearly three weeks."

"I haven't been avoiding you. Even though we're living on the same ranch, our paths just haven't crossed. I came especially to check on you tonight, so get off your sibling rivalry horse and talk to me," Trey said.

She went back to work. "I'm not trying to prove anything. I don't like being broke, and if I want money I have to work for it, so you'll have to talk to me while I work. I can't afford to stop and visit."

"You've been rising at five to help Roseanna with breakfast and working until eleven-thirty at the lodge, then going to the police station until eight, and rushing out to the stables when you get home to work until eleven or after. That boils down to less than six hours of sleep. That's not healthy."

She pushed the wheelbarrow past him and out the back door to the fertilizer pile. "Maybe not but it makes the time pass quickly. So how's teaching going?" she asked when she returned and started another stall. Suddenly giving him a piece of her mind wasn't so important. She was so glad to see blood kin she could have hugged him, but then he'd have the edge and she wasn't willing to give him that—not just yet.

"I did this job a few times," he said.

"Bravo for you," she said.

"Teaching is fine. It's more than fine. I've found my place in the world, Greta. I love the peace and contentment here. I love my job for the first time in my life. And Rosy and I are happy. I'm hoping you can find the same thing," Trey said.

"I will someday but not here."

"You might be surprised." Trey smiled.

Seeing Greta do menial labor was the strangest thing he'd ever experienced. He kept fighting the urge to pinch himself to make sure he wasn't dreaming. "I'm on my way home. Had a late meeting at the school so I'm just now getting home. See you around. Do you need anything?"

"Not now. I could have used your bank account three weeks ago to pay my bail, but I'm managing. If you have any clout with time, you could make it pass quickly. Come back and visit. I'm here most evenings."

Trey waved and headed out the double doors at the end of the horse barn. Greta didn't watch him go. She finished thirty minutes later in record time. It was only ten-thirty. She'd catch an extra hour of sleep tonight.

Hopefully without dreams.

It was at least six city blocks from the barn to the house. The night breezes were still hot but at least they didn't smell like horses. She kept to the gravel road that led from the lodge to the very back of the ranch where Roseanna and Trey had put their double-wide on an acre of land. A raccoon crossed her path at one point and a possum eyed her from the side of the road, but she didn't let either of them frighten her. The first time she'd made the journey from barn to lodge she'd had a standoff with a skunk. It wouldn't budge and she was too frightened to move for fear it would spray her. After that she scouted a different pathway that led to the back door instead of the front one and vowed she wouldn't let anything terrorize her again.

"Miss Greta?" a deep voice said from the end of the porch about the time she opened the door.

"Who is it?" she asked.

"It's Fred. The others have gone to bed. Come and talk to me." It was the youngest of six fisherman who'd booked the lodge for a week. They'd arrived Sunday night in time for supper and planned to leave Friday right after breakfast.

Guests were the reason Greta had to rise at five instead of seven for the whole week. Roseanna started cooking at five-thirty, and breakfast was put on the sideboard at seven every morning. Roseanna told her that breakfast depended on the clientele. Big old burly fishermen and hunters liked a full he-man meal to start off the day, so they'd made gravy, scrambled egg casserole, hot biscuits, and slabs of ham every morning.

"Sorry, Fred. A long hot shower is waiting for me," she said.

In a few easy strides the man crossed the porch and held the door shut. "Five minutes. Just talk to me five minutes."

The same fear that the skunk caused was back in full force. Roseanna had gone home after supper. Greta was alone. "Why?"

"Because I think you are a lovely lady and I want to know what's going on here. Is that cop who brings you home every night your boyfriend?"

"No, he is not!" Greta said quickly, then thought better. "He's not my boyfriend. He's my fiancé. We work together at the police station. I'm a secretary and he's on the force. I wrecked my car a few weeks ago and he's been giving me a ride until I can get it fixed."

Fred let go of the door. "Well, if you ever see through his arrogance, you just call me." He slowly slipped a card into the pocket of the T-shirt she wore. "I think you and I'd get along real good."

"What about your wife, Fred?" she asked.

Fred chuckled. "Get rid of the fiancé and give me a call. Lots of things can change and I can give you the life you ought to have. Woman like you shouldn't be working at all. You should be living in the lap of luxury. I can provide that. Penthouse apartment in Houston. Little sports car or a limo with your own driver. Credit cards to use at any shop. You name it and it's yours."

"Good night, Fred." Greta slipped inside the house and almost ran to her bedroom. After the quickest shower she'd ever taken, she wrapped up in a terry robe that covered her body from neck to toes. She peeked out into the hallway. No one lurked around and everything seemed quiet. Fred was either in his room or still on the porch. She scurried down the hall and locked the bedroom door behind her. After she dressed for bed, she removed the card from the pocket of her dirty T-shirt and tore it to shreds. Two more mornings and he'd be gone. She'd use the different path to come home tomorrow night and go in the lodge by the kitchen door.

"All skunks are not black and white," she whispered as she pulled the covers up to her chin. "But then, maybe they are." She thought of the silver streaks in Fred's jet-black hair and his light gray eyes. Maybe he was a descendant of nothing more than the common skunk.

"You look like you didn't sleep too well. Got bags under your eyes. Been working too late? Need a little more beauty sleep?" Jodie said in the morning.

Greta reached for an apron and covered a yawn with the back of her hand. "You got that right, but beauty sleep doesn't bring in a paycheck on Friday."

Roseanna browned sausage in a cast-iron skillet and wore a bibbed gingham apron over jeans and a bright yellow T-shirt. Her brown hair was tied at the nape of her neck with a ribbon that matched the shirt. With her long legs and flawless complexion, she could have picked up work at any modeling agency. She sure didn't look like she belonged in a kitchen at five-thirty in the morning.

Jodie rolled out dough and cut perfect little biscuit circles. Her red shirt was worn but clean, and her jeans only had one hole in the hip pocket. Her boots had seen better days but she swore they were barely broken in. She was almost as pretty as Roseanna and several inches taller, but Greta couldn't see her walking down a runway in a designer outfit. Jodie could be decked out in a Stella McCartney dress and Prada shoes and she'd still walk like she'd just come off the tractor.

"Then I've got bad news and good news. Bad news is your paycheck will be a little short this week. Good news is you can get some sleep tonight. Daddy and

Momma are home from visiting our aunt in southeast Oklahoma and Daddy's going to finish up the hay job. I'll do the stables and you can have a night off."

Greta sighed in relief. She'd spend the whole evening in her room with the door locked.

Rosy narrowed her eyes at Greta. "What's that sigh all about? I thought you wanted to work all the hours you could to make the time pass quicker."

"I did, but I had a problem last night with one of the boarders. Fred tried to proposition me. Offered to make me his mistress, or at least that's the way I took it. Mentioned an apartment and credit cards and anything I wanted. I suppose there's another side to the story and he'd expect some kind of payment for all those things. He asked me if Kyle was my boyfriend. I lied and said he was my fiancé, so if you two could back me up this morning and tomorrow, I'd appreciate it. I'll just go straight up to my room when I get home this evening and stay there."

"I'll throw him out," Roseanna said.

Greta began shredding a pound block of American cheese in the food processor. "No, it would make a bigger problem than just keeping up the pretense."

Jodie's eyes twinkled. "You going to tell Kyle you're engaged?"

"Not unless I have to," Greta said.

She had to.

That evening when he delivered her back to the lodge, Fred was sitting on the porch. Kyle insisted on walking her right up to the door every evening and Fred was a stick of dynamite with the match kissing the fuse. He might sit there with a smirk on his face or he could ask when they were getting married. She couldn't take a chance on blowing her cover story.

"Please sit here just a minute, Kyle. Don't open the door just yet. I've got a great big problem and I need your help."

"Whew, it must be a matter of life or death if you are asking my help. What is it?"

"See that boarder over there on the porch?" She told him what had happened the night before.

"And you told him I was your boyfriend?" Kyle almost choked on the words.

Greta pursed her mouth and grimaced. "Worse. I told him you're my fiancé. He's leaving right after breakfast tomorrow morning so if you could pretend just for this one time. Kiss me on the cheek. Say something that will convince him we are really engaged."

"Isn't that a wedding band I see on the hand with the cigarette?" Kyle asked.

"Yes, he's married. I think he was offering to make me his mistress. He mentioned a sports car, an apartment, and credit cards with no limits, but he didn't mention a divorce. He's slimier than those drunks you bring to the jail."

"I'll do one better. I'm off duty. I'll beat the—"

"No. Just play along and I'll go up to my room and read a book all evening."

"Are you sure you are safe in the house with him, Greta? Etta would have him out on his ear if she knew."

"I know that, but she and Roxie are in Las Vegas for the week. They're taking in all the shows and playing the slots. Rosy says they're going a lot now that they've lost their other friend. What was her name?"

"Molly Brannon. Cancer got her last year. Okay, let's go do an acting job. But you're going to owe me for this one."

"You ever been married, Kyle? Would you do that to your wife?"

"I'm twenty-eight years old and my daddy would take me to the wood shed even yet if I did. And no, I've never been married, Greta. Never even thought about it. When I find a woman who'll make me feel like Momma does Daddy, I might consider it after we've dated two or three years."

"What am I going to owe you? Maybe the price is too high for your acting services," she asked as he opened the car door for her.

He held out his hand and she put hers into it. "I'll think of something."

Heat that had nothing to do with the weather flowed through his fingertips all the way up her arm. She felt high color rising in her cheeks when he led her across the yard, swinging her hand as they walked.

"Evening, Fred. How was the fishing?" she asked as nonchalantly as possible.

"Didn't catch a thing," he said. "Hello, Officer. I understand the two of you are making wedding plans. Congratulations."

"That's right," Kyle said.

Great Lord Almighty, I'm glad I told him what was going on before we got out of the car, she thought. *Fred must have not believed a word I said last night. I thought I was a better liar than that. Kyle would have been sputtering like a volcano about to erupt about now if I hadn't told him.*

"When's the big day?"

"Day after Thanksgiving," Kyle said. "Wanted to get her a little diamond ring but she said she'd rather have matching gold wedding bands. So we've got them on layaway over at Jones Jewelry in Davis. Kind of like the one you're wearing there. She's a practical girl. Said she'd rather have a new washing machine than a fancy diamond. I'm getting a good woman, don't you think?"

Fred put his cigarette butt in the container Etta provided for smokers. "I'm sure you are. Hope you two are real happy."

"Oh, we will be," Greta said.

Kyle leaned forward and kissed her on the forehead. "Well, darlin', go on in and get your work boots. I'll wait right here."

Suddenly Greta wanted to kick him in the shins. She'd only wanted him to escort her past Fred, pretend a few minutes, and leave.

"She's going to help me feed the cattle tonight and then we're watching a movie at my house," Kyle explained to Fred.

She glared at him and envisioned stealing his gun and shooting him and Fred both right there on the porch. She could have the blood cleaned up before Roseanna arrived to cook breakfast. She might even have both bodies dragged off and sunk in the pond. The catfish would have a good supper. Etta would never have to know. His fishing buddies could be convinced he went home a day early.

Fred was leaning on her bedroom doorjamb and startled her when she slung open the door. "If you were mine I wouldn't waste your beauty feeding cows and watching movies on a DVD player. We'd be dining in a fine restaurant this evening. You'd be wearing Versace and diamonds. And we'd be attending a Broadway production."

"No thank you." Greta shut her door and kept walking. All the things Wilma said that first day she'd worked in the station came back to mind. The man had just offered her everything she'd told Wilma she wanted in a mate, yet he made her skin crawl like it was covered in a million mosquitoes.

"Had a problem there. He said he needed another pack of cigarettes from his room and I couldn't very well follow him. Is everything all right? Are you ready?" Kyle asked from the porch swing.

"Oh, yes." Greta nodded.

Kyle slipped an arm around her shoulders. "Did he say anything?"

"Just reminded me of what I could have. He didn't touch me, though."

Kyle didn't know why he was angry. "Did he last night?"

"Barely. He put his card in my T-shirt pocket and was very careful not to touch any part of me, but even that gave me a case of the willies. So is this a farce or am I really going to have to help feed cattle?"

"Payment. I told you I'd think of something. You can drive the truck and I'll do the feeding."

"Oh, no I can't. I'm not allowed to drive until my community service is over," she reminded him.

"Okay then. I'll do the chores. You can mow my lawn," he said.

She wondered if he'd start the mower for her. She'd never done lawn work in her life. "Then we'll be even?"

"Right after the movie. I told lies enough that I'll have to pray real hard before I go to sleep tonight as it is. We will watch a movie before I drive you back home tonight. That way I won't be telling still yet another one."

He drove through the park and continued on north, past the place where she'd had the wreck, before he turned back to the east. "My place is back here. Not a lot unlike Trey and Rosy's. I bought ten acres from my dad when I started to work for the force. Put a trailer on it and it's home."

She stared at the single-wide trailer house set in the middle of a white picket-fenced yard. At least six cats lazed around on the redwood deck that served as a front porch. Two hounds bounded from under the deck to greet Kyle before he had time to open the car door.

"Hey, Scarlett and Melanie, how did your day go?" He talked to them as if they were human.

"You must like *Gone with the Wind*." She didn't wait for him but slung the door open for herself.

"No, Momma does. She named the dogs when they were puppies. They were part of the deal when I bought the acres. I had to take the dogs if I wanted to live on the place."

"Why?"

"Because she wanted two more puppies and Dad said she couldn't have four dogs. Have you had supper?"

"No, I usually grab leftovers from the fridge when I get to the lodge," she said.

"Good, because I'm hungry. You can make something while the dogs and I do the chores," he said.

She arched an eyebrow toward him. "Is that the payment too?"

"No, it's because we're both hungry. I'm going to change clothes and it'll take about an hour for me to get things done. By then surely you can roust up some grub of some kind."

"I don't cook very well," she admitted.

"Can you fry an egg?"

"I can make an omelet," she said.

"Then you can cook. Make yourself at home. It'll just take a few minutes for me to change into my work clothes." He left her on the porch with six cats rubbing around her ankles and went inside the trailer.

He appeared a few minutes later in tight Wranglers, worn boots, and a snowy white T-shirt only slightly frayed around the neck. "See you as soon as I can."

After he rumbled down a lane in his big black pickup truck with both dogs in the back, the wind blowing their ears back and their tongues lolling out, she cautiously opened the front door and went inside. No more animals greeted her. The back side of the trailer's living room had been removed and replaced with glass doors leading out on another huge deck that overlooked a pond. Fishing equipment propped against the railing testified that Kyle did fish right off the deck. A deep brown suede sofa was positioned so she could watch the ducks swimming on the pond. A matching chair and ottoman looked to have been used more than the sofa. It must be Kyle's choice for watching television or reading. She picked up the book on the side table. So he liked John Grisham also.

Like most trailers, the kitchen was right off the living room. His mother must have had a hand in decorating it because crisp yellow curtains hung on the two windows: one overlooking the front deck, the other the side yard. Was he serious about her mowing the yard? He hadn't mentioned it again and she sure wasn't going to bring up the subject. Maybe cooking supper would pay her bill in full.

She opened the refrigerator. Big brown eggs waited in a bowl. His folks must have chickens. Feeling a bit skittish about prowling, she opened the cabinet doors to find everything she needed. All the spices she used plus some she'd never heard of. What on earth did a bachelor do with dill weed? She could have shouted when she found Bisquick. The only way she knew how to make a biscuit was with the premix. Potatoes were in the drawer of the refrigerator so they could have hash browns with the omelets.

By the time he walked through the door she had food ready and waiting. He washed his hands and face in the kitchen sink and pulled out a chair to the small table. "Smells delicious. I love breakfast food for supper. Seldom take the time to make myself a big meal in the mornings. You want to say grace or should I?"

She sat down and laid the paper napkin across her lap. "Why did you ask?"

"Momma calls grace. She says who's going to say it at each meal. I guess it's just habit for me to look to the lady of the house," he said.

Greta blushed. She wasn't the lady of this trailer house and never would be. "You go ahead." She dropped her head, shut her eyes tightly, and didn't look up until she heard him say, "Amen."

"Mmmm." He made appreciative noises. "You cook anything else?"

"I make a mean bologna sandwich."

"That all?"

"Roseanna's been teaching me a few things at the lodge. I could probably open a can of soup or make a grilled cheese sandwich if I was starving."

"I don't believe it. This is almost as good as Momma's breakfast. These are Bisquick biscuits aren't they?"

"Yes, they are."

He chuckled. "Momma has always used that stuff for biscuits. Daddy says her scratch biscuits are dangerous. A man carrying one in his lunch bucket could go to jail for toting around a concealed weapon."

She had to smile. These backwoods country people did have a way with words.

He buttered another biscuit. "I reckon supper is enough of a payment for me having to be engaged to the likes of you. You don't have to mow the lawn. Besides, it's almost dark. We'll watch a movie and then I'll take you home and walk you to your bedroom door. When I hear the lock I'll feel a lot safer. Fred is sure some piece of work, isn't he?"

"What movie?"

"I got a whole selection over there. I'll help with the cleanup in here and then we'll choose one."

Hands brushed against other hands, hips bumped into other hips, and thoughts went toward things other than movies. Greta wanted to keep a shred of anger wrapped around her heart and soul, but it kept slipping away. She didn't like Kyle or his caveman attitude, but then he'd say something funny and she'd forget that she was mad at him.

In her previous world she wouldn't even be in this place. She would never ever watch a movie with a man in a trailer house of any kind. If he didn't have the wherewithal to take her to dinner and then to a fancy theater, she wouldn't have given him a second look. She'd chewed men up with a lot less to offer than Kyle Parsons, and yet, she was actually enjoying an evening with him.

"So what will it be? I've got *Lethal Weapon*, all four of them. I've got . . ."

"Chick flicks?" she asked.

He rolled his eyes and one little thread of anger appeared. He'd said they'd choose together and already he was showing his male superiority by wanting to watch blood and guts. She was surprised he didn't say he had recorded tapes of wrestling or football.

"Here's *Steel Magnolias* and *While You Were Sleeping*. I didn't buy them. My sister left them here last time she brought her daughter for a visit."

"I'm sure you didn't purchase them so don't get your boxers in a bind. I've never seen *While You Were Sleeping*. But we don't have to watch it, Kyle. It's already ten o'clock. I'm sure I could just go home now."

He appeared more than a little relieved. "By the time I get you there and in your room, it *would* be bedtime. The movie won't end until almost midnight."

"Then let's call it a night."

"Okay, but some other time you are welcome to come watch this thing while I fish," he said.

"Sure thing." Greta would never set foot in his trailer again. This was a onetime deal. Even if he did make her heart thump around an extra time or two when he touched her hand or backed into her in the kitchen. It was simply because she hadn't dated in a long time. When she got back to Tulsa or Dallas, whichever way she decided to go, she'd definitely have to get back into the dating world.

Chapter Seven

Greta sat at the end of the kitchen table, a glass of cold sweet tea in front of her, listening to the latest gossip on everyone in Murray County. Roxie flittered about, preparing potato salad and checking the baked beans. She wore white spandex pants that stopped mid-calf, a brilliant pink tank top covered with a sheer overshirt printed with bright-colored parrots. Her hot pink high-heeled shoes made clicking noises on the highly waxed tile floor. Etta fussed around making three of her famous chocolate sheet cakes. She was Roxie's opposite, most days looking like the farm wife and inn owner she was, but today she'd spruced up with stretch denim jeans, red Nikes, and a red, white, and blue striped knit shirt.

Greta felt more than a little underdressed in her hand-me-down jeans and plain white T-shirt. She had taken time to put on makeup and style her hair, but she wore a pair of two-dollar yellow flip-flops she'd bought at Wal-Mart. More than feeling like a pauper at a ball, she felt like a third wheel.

Roseanna had Trey and the bloom was most definitely not off the marriage. She kept stealing glances out the back window and he'd look up often with a wave and a wink. Maybe Trey had found his niche in life after all. Perhaps he'd had one of those near-death experiences when he'd been kidnapped and chained to a tree that caused him to look at life, love, and possessions in a different light. If so, Greta wished him all the best.

Sincerely.

That idea brought her up short and she stared at Roseanna from her peripheral vision. Rosy was lovely with her dark green eyes and long brown hair, but it was her height most people noticed. That and those long, long legs. Must be what attracted Trey to her in the beginning. They were still mismatched. Rosy in her jeans and dark green tank top looked like she was about to embark on another rescue mission. Trey in his perfectly creased trousers and casual three-button shirt looked as if he was on his way to play golf.

Jodie was telling a story about someone Jack Brewer had been engaged to at one time. The woman had married another man and he was running for city councilman in Sulphur. Roxie laughed and declared that wasn't any big surprise, and if Jack had married her, he'd be doing the same.

Dee pulled up a rocking chair and held her son, eight-month-old Jaxson, while he slept. Dee wasn't very tall and built on the slim side. She had light brown hair and big brown eyes and delicate features that would have probably landed her an acting job if she'd been in Hollywood instead of Murray County, Oklahoma. She was Roxie's granddaughter and lived in a trailer house next door to Roxie's Bed-and-Breakfast, the first B&B of three to retire in the recent past.

The kitchen door flew open and two more people arrived.

"Stella, come on in here," Jodie said.

"Rance, the guys are out at the smoker doing manly things." Dee motioned. "Get you a glass of tea before you go. Weatherman didn't miss his guess when he said we'd have a hot one today."

"Hey, wait a minute," Etta said. "Need to make you acquainted with Trey's sister, Greta. She's staying at the lodge until Thanksgiving. Greta, this is Stella and Rance Harper. They live next door to Molly's old B&B, the Brannon Inn. Stella ran it for a while and now her sister takes care of it. Where are Maggie and Lauren today?"

Stella opened the refrigerator door and shoved a platter of deviled eggs and a layered dessert that looked a lot like banana pudding inside. "They're over at Momma's. Nice to meet you, Greta. I believe I saw you at Rosy and Trey's reception. How do you like this area?"

Greta wasn't sure how to answer.

"She hates it but she's a trooper. I think she's going to survive," Jodie said.

"Pleasure meeting you, Greta." Rance waved and joined the men in the backyard.

Stella raised an eyebrow.

"Haven't you heard the gossip?" Jodie asked. "Greta is the one who was driving too fast and talking on her cell phone. She lost control of the car and Kyle Parsons . . ."

Stella's big blue eyes widened. "Oh my gosh, that was you?"

"That was me," Greta said.

Stella was every bit as tall as Rosy. She wore white walking shorts and a cute little red blouse with white polka dots and a pair of sandals that were either a designer brand or a dang good knockoff.

Before the conversation could go any further, the back door opened again and another tall blonde came inside. "Hello, everyone," she said. "Where do I put these pecan pies, Roxie?"

Roxie pointed to an area on the counter top. "Right there. And let me make you known."

The lady glanced around the room. She pointed toward Greta. "I know everyone but you. I'm Tally, Dee's sister. And that child out there already bugging those men to take her fishing is my daughter, Bodine. My husband, Ken, is the one in the lawn chair beside her."

"I'm Greta Fields, Trey's sister," Greta said.

The look on Tally's face said she'd already heard tales about Greta. She looked at Rosy and Jodie.

"It's all right. We've called a truce. She has to stay in the country until Thanksgiving, so we've decided to forego murder and mayhem until after that." Rosy laughed.

"But not thoughts of it on occasion," Jodie admitted.

Greta forced a smile. Jodie had no idea how right she was.

Tally poured a glass of tea and joined the women around the table. "Okay, catch me up. What are you doing here until Thanksgiving? And give me that baby, Dee. You get to hold him all the time."

Dee carefully handed over Jaxson, who nuzzled right down into his aunt's arms and continued to sleep.

Greta gave her the short form of the story.

"You killed Kyle's bull? It's a wonder you're still breathing. And Granny Etta, how come you went down there and got her out of county lockup? Roxie made me spend a year."

Roxie patted her on the shoulder and pulled up a chair. "You needed it. She was a three-time loser, Greta. Had an addiction to the Indian Casinos and wrote some hot checks for the third time to pay for her gambling. I figured a year in county would cure or kill her. Either one beat the heck out of the way she was living."

"Tough old buzzard, isn't she?" Tally laughed. "So what are you doing while you wait out your time, Greta?"

"The judge laid down the law. I have to work for Etta four hours a day for my room and board, then Kyle takes me to the police station where I work for Wilma from noon to eight for community service. Then I come home and work for Jodie when she has something for me to do so I can make some real money," Greta answered honestly.

Tally raised both eyebrows and sputtered. "Kyle?"

"Yes, the judge evidently has a sense of humor," Greta said.

"So what do you think of Kyle Parsons?"

"She told him he couldn't tame me and I was a kitten compared to her," Rosy said.

Tally giggled. "Is that true?"

"That I said it or that I am?" Greta asked.

"Both."

"Yes, it is," Greta said.

"And she's telling the truth," Jodie said.

"But I'm not as mean as Jodie." Greta defended herself.

"Nobody is that mean." Dee laughed.

"Oh, come on, girls. I'm just hard to please when it comes to men folks. And you all had to follow your broken road back home where you belonged. I never left so I don't have to learn the lessons you did."

"Broken road?" Greta asked. Kyle had mentioned that same thing the other night when they were talking.

"Sure. You ever heard that Rascal Flatts song about the broken road?" Stella asked.

Greta nodded.

"Well, every one of us here can relate to that song. Let me bring you up to snuff on my story. I married a wannabe actor and wound up in Hollywood for a few years in a miserable relationship. Granny Molly died and left me the inn with the stipulation I couldn't sell it for several years. Mitch, my ex-husband, was so angry that he couldn't get at that money, he left me. I came home and settled into a comfortable rut of running the inn. Then Rance Harper appeared one day. Quite literally I backed right into him. We fought with the commitment word for several months. I wanted a lifetime thing and he wanted a mistress. So to make the long story short, my broken roads finally led me right back home to Murray County to a happy marriage with that handsome hunk out there in the tight blue jeans and cowboy hat," Stella said.

"My broken road did the same. I came home to Roxie's and fell in love with Jack," Dee said. "He'd been my best friend our whole lives and now he's even more."

Greta held up a hand. "Just a minute. I've got a question that has nothing to do with the broken road stories. Why do you all call Roxie by her name? Isn't she your real grandmother?"

"Oh, yes, but . . ." Tally looked at the other ladies.

They said in unison, "God and General Lee have titles. Everyone else has a name."

Greta laughed with them. She already respected Roxie but now she liked her even more.

"My turn now. I didn't do the perfect circle. My broken road took a side trip to Nashville, played around in Memphis and a dozen other places before it came home to rest," Tally said.

"You know my story," Roseanna said.

"Well, my road doesn't end here. God, I'd shoot myself between the eyes if it did. I'm going to Dallas or Tulsa as soon as the judge gives me back my driver's license and rights to a cell phone." Greta almost shuddered at the thought of living in Murray County all her life.

"Never know what might happen," Etta said.

"So there's nothing between you and Kyle?" Dee asked.

Greta shook her head emphatically. "Not one thing. Never could be. We're so different, it would never, ever work."

"Speak of the devil and he shall appear. Yesterday after church I invited him to come spend the day with us," Roxie said. "His momma and daddy are off to see his sisters and he didn't have any plans. I'm sure glad there's nothing between you two, Greta. I'd feel bad if I'd caused a problem."

"That man hasn't got two healthy brain cells in his good-looking head if he thinks he can lasso in Greta Fields. She's got more sense than that," Jodie said. "There won't be a problem here today unless you're trying to play matchmaker between him and me, Roxie."

"Girl, I'm brave but I'm not an idiot. Kyle is not for

you. Even if you two do have the same background and interests, he's not the man for you."

"Who is?" Etta asked with a twinkle in her eyes.

"Okay, Jodie, you're in the hot seat. Tell us what kind of feller you hope for," Rosy said.

Jodie didn't stutter one bit. "Me? If I had to hope, it would be for someone totally different than Trey Fields. Someone who wears his jeans tight and the right length to stack over his well-polished cowboy boots, who sits a horse like he was born on one and who can pull a calf without gagging. And then he has to make me feel like I'm a queen but not give in to me so much that he's not the king of the double-wide. He has to stand up for himself even if it makes me mad and he has to love me with his whole heart. That's who I'd hope for if I was to hope."

"And you, Greta? You are the other unmarried lass here today. What kind of man do you dream about?" Etta asked.

That was the second time Greta had been asked the same question. She paused a moment before speaking. "Well, it isn't Kyle Parsons. I want the opposite of Jodie's dreamboat. I want a man who has a closet full of Armani suits, who has a limo and a driver to take him to work, a staff to keep his house and grounds, and maybe a jet to fly me anywhere I want to go."

"Whew!" Stella laughed. "That's a big order, but what kind of man is he? You told us what you want to own, not what he's like."

"He has to . . ."

Kyle popped his head in the back door. "Hi, ladies. Roxie, I'm spitting dust. Mind if I make myself an iced tea?"

Roxie pointed toward the tea pitcher. "Go right ahead. Make yourself at home, Kyle."

"What are you doing here?" he blurted out when he saw Greta.

"Same thing you are," she snapped.

He set his jaw, poured his tea, and left without another word.

Dee started the giggle. Stella joined. Tally tried to keep from shaking so she wouldn't wake the baby. Jodie was the first one to guffaw and then the whole place broke into laughter.

All but Greta.

"I wouldn't be so sure that your road doesn't lead you right back to Murray County when the time comes, Greta," Roxie said.

"The day I live here permanently the *Daily Oklahoman*'s headlines will say *Hell Finally Froze Over.*"

Greta found herself enjoying the day with the eclectic mix of people. Kyle kept his distance and the few times he even glanced her way, it was with indifference, which was fine with her.

Tally's daughter, Bodine, sat beside her at supper, which was served family style like they did at the lodge. Immediately after Jack asked grace, Bodine piped up. "So I hear you told some man at the lodge you were engaged to Kyle. Is that the best you could do? Lord, I could have spun a better story than that. I'd have told him I was marrying Brad Pitt next week."

Greta shot Kyle a drop-dead-on-the-spot look.

He held up his hands in defense.

Bodine picked up the platter of deviled eggs, helped herself to three, and passed them to her left. "Oh, don't get your Hanes Her Way in a bind. Kyle didn't tell it. Etta told me when we were playing Scrabble a while ago. I just can't imagine why you'd choose him to be fake-engaged to. He's a cop. You couldn't get away with anything."

"Bodine has been encouraged to speak her mind," Roxie explained. "She hasn't grown up enough to know when not to, though."

"Truth is, I couldn't tell the man at the lodge who was trying to talk me into running way with him that I was engaged to Brad Pitt. He'd seen Kyle bringing me home from work every day, so he asked me if he was my boyfriend," Greta explained.

The whole table was dead silent.

"I'd have told him he was my brother before I'd have admitted I was engaged to Kyle," Bodine said.

Still no one said a word.

"And what's so wrong with me?" Kyle asked.

"You really want to know?" Bodine asked.

"Maybe not in front of everyone but maybe you could tell me later." Kyle actually blushed. Good grief, what could be so drastically wrong with him that Bodine kept on and on about it?

"I was just jerking your chain." Bodine laughed. "I'm jealous that Greta got to pretend you were her honey bear. I'd always thought maybe when I got grown I'd marry you just to prove to Roseanna that I was smarter than her."

Two bright spots of high color filled Kyle's cheeks.

Greta came close to spitting tea across the table.

Roseanna looked at Trey, who shrugged.

Jodie laughed.

Roxie narrowed her eyes at her great-granddaughter. "Bodine, do you want me to take you to the woodshed?"

"Roxie, I didn't say a single cuss word," Bodine protested.

Roxie's chin quivered but she kept the laughter inside. "I guess you didn't. Now let's go on to something else. Tell me, Tally, how are classes going?"

Greta was thankful the spotlight was off her for a while. She listened as Tally entertained everyone with stories of her college classes and the students in them. Then the conversation went off in another direction. Before long, Greta had polished off two plates of food, an oversized chunk of pecan pie, and a small piece of chocolate sheet cake.

When Kyle pushed away from the table with a groan, she surely felt like doing the same thing.

"I'm going to have to take a walk or . . ."

"Not until you've watched the sunset from the back porch," Bodine said. "You know the rules, Kyle. If I can't go fishing until the sunset-watching is finished, you're not going to go for a walk."

"We'll do cleanup." Tally motioned for Ken to help. "Dee, you and Jack make the lemonade and the rest of you can go on to the back porch. We won't be long. Bodine, you can help in here."

"Ahhh." Bodine wrinkled her pert little nose and made a face.

"Pull that curly hair up in a ponytail and let's get it over with so we can go see if the bass are biting at Buckhorn," Ken whispered.

Bodine had carried half the leftovers to the kitchen before Roxie and the rest of the folks made it out the door. If she hurried, maybe the sunset would do the same and she'd still have time for a couple of hours of fishing.

Roxie patted the chair next to hers for Greta. "Maybe I'd better explain about lemonade and sunsets. Way back when my late husband was still alive, when we first got married, we saved an hour a day for sunsets. After supper we'd take our lemonade to the back porch and sit together for an hour, sometimes more, but never less, and tell each other all about our day. When he died, I kept up the habit. It's my favorite part of the day. Dee and Jack come over every night and whoever else wants to join us is welcome. Our friends have an open invitation. This place is called Roxie's B&B. Legally that stands for Roxie's Bed-and-Breakfast, but it also stands for Roxie's Bellyachin' and Blessin's. Today is one of the blessin's days."

"Why did you paint it red?" Greta wondered if she'd said the words aloud the moment they escaped into the air.

"Want to answer that?" Roxie asked Dee, who carried two pitchers of fresh-squeezed lemonade out the door.

"I asked the same question when I came home from Pennsylvania almost two years ago. Thought it was the most gawdawful sight I'd ever seen. Roxie told me God made the cardinal and I could get used to it. It grows on you. I wouldn't change the color for anything now."

Greta thought she was entirely too full to drink the whole glass of lemonade and was surprised when the sun set that she was holding an empty glass. Bodine and Ken left with their fishing rods. Tally took a book upstairs to study for a test the next day. Stella and Rance headed out to her mother's and took Roseanna and Trey with them. Etta went home while Greta was in the bathroom.

Greta looked forlornly at the empty back porch, searching for someone going back to the lodge.

"Guess I'll have to take you home," Roxie said.

"I can take her." Kyle heard the comment as he came back from a twenty-minute walk down the road toward the Buckhorn area of the Lake of the Arbuckles.

"You're going that way anyhow," Roxie said.

"Yes, I am. You ready, Greta?"

"I am." She nodded. "Thank you, Roxie, for a lovely day. It's the first time I've had a holiday since the wreck and I've really enjoyed it."

"Come around anytime. Etta comes over often. Hitch a ride with her and keep me posted on whether you change your mind about our little chunk of the world," Roxie said.

"I'll do it, but the days of miracles are over." Greta waved good-bye as she rounded the end of the house and headed toward Kyle's pickup.

When they reached the lodge, he walked her to the door as usual, said he'd see her the next day, as usual, then stopped.

"What?" she asked when he didn't turn around to leave.

"Nothing."

"You looked like you wanted to say something," she said.

"It's nothing. It doesn't matter and it was a long time ago."

"I don't need a boring story to put me to sleep tonight. The only thing I need is a long soaking bath and then I'm going to reread *The Pelican Brief* for the umpteenth time."

"I just finished rereading it for at least the third or fourth time. Love that book." He leaned forward and for a brief second Greta thought he'd kiss her. In that minimoment she wondered what it would be like to have his lips on hers, to be wrapped up in his arms.

The moment passed and he backed away.

"I'll see you at noon tomorrow." He threw over his shoulder as he left.

She waved and shivered in spite of the heat. Something down deep in her heart said that she'd wanted Kyle Parsons to kiss her, and that scared her worse than the stupid dream about her father giving her to him without even asking if she wanted to go.

Chapter Eight

"Hey, Kyle, you got your radio on?" A voice filled the cab of the pickup truck just before Kyle turned back south at the park entrance to take Greta home that Friday evening.

He pushed a button and turned his head to one side. "I'm here. What do you need?"

"Got a domestic in progress. Neighbors called it in. Lassitors at it again, out by the deaf school. Everyone else is tied up. I'm punching you back in. You are now on the clock."

"Just what I wanted to do tonight. I missed the kick-off and by the time I get you home and this taken care of . . ." Kyle grumbled.

The dispatcher's voice cut his sentence short.

"Kyle, the neighbor called again. They're out in the

front yard and they've each got a butcher knife. Hurry up!"

He floored the gas pedal and shot straight ahead, tapped the brake enough to slide around the corner in front of the Baptist church, and barely looked both ways at the stop signs before gassing it again. At the next corner, he glanced at Greta sitting in the passenger's seat.

"Guess you're going with me, but you are going to sit in the truck and not make a noise. Is that understood?" he snapped as he stopped abruptly in front of a small white frame house.

True to the dispatcher's message, two people were out on the lawn with an enormous yellow rosebush between them. Fading light flickered off knife blades.

Kyle jumped out of the truck before she had time to agree or disagree. "Okay, I want you to both put those weapons away," he demanded.

The man stopped yelling and circling the rosebush long enough to glance Kyle's way. "Don't you be telling me what to do. This hussy says she's going to divorce me this time, but she's not taking Riggs with her. I'll kill her before I see her take my baby out of this house."

"Come on, Henry, put the knife down and let's talk about this. Minnie, you aren't going to hurt Henry so why don't you hand me your knife and then Henry will put his down and we'll talk."

"Stupid old fool might chase after everything that's wearin' a skirt tail but he's not taking Riggs. I raised that cat from a half-starved kitten. You better stay away from me, old man. I'll bury this up in your fat gizzard. You ain't takin' Riggs. You wouldn't even remember to feed him, you'd be so busy out runnin' after the women."

Kyle eased the flashlight from his belt and took two steps forward. "Henry, I'm asking you one more time to either put that knife down or hand it to me."

"And I'm tellin' you for the last time to get in your truck and get out of here. This ain't got a thing to do with you. It's mine and Minnie's fight on our own land. Once I kill her, then it's your business."

Kyle stepped closer and knocked the knife from Henry's hand with the flashlight and deftly had him handcuffed before the man could say a single cuss word. Greta was mentally congratulating him on his victory when she saw Minnie's shoulders quiver in laughter. A scream filled the air as she raised the butcher knife and started toward Henry, now sitting on the ground with handcuffs keeping him from defending himself.

A sudden jolt of adrenaline rushed through Greta's veins. She slung open the truck door and bounded across the short space, grabbing Minnie's hand a split second before she could plunge the knife into Henry's bald head.

Kyle turned quickly, closing his hand around Greta's as she stayed the blade from doing fatal damage. It took both of them to wrestle the knife away from the skinny woman's hand and handcuff her hands behind her.

She turned on Kyle. "You played dirty. I was about to finish this problem once and for all."

"You can tell that to the judge when he gets around to talking to you," Kyle said. "Right now you are both going to jail. Minnie, I'm charging you with attempted murder. Henry, I'm charging you with whatever I can find in the book to throw at you. Shame on the both of you, acting like this."

"Don't you be shamin' nobody. You ain't old enough to shame me," Minnie said. "And I'll tell that judge what I think of him too. Go get Riggs out of the house. I can't leave him in there all night by hisself. He'll cry. If I've got to go to jail then my cat is going with me."

He grabbed Henry's arm and led him toward the truck. "I'm not getting Riggs. You are each entitled to one phone call when you get to jail. You can call someone to take care of your cat or call a lawyer. I don't care. Come on."

Minnie took off in a stumbling run toward the house. "Riggs, baby, come here to Momma."

"Get her," Kyle yelled back at Greta.

By the time Greta reached the woman she'd already turned around backwards and was attempting to open the screen door with her cuffed hands. Greta shoved a foot against the door and grabbed her arm. "Come on with me, lady. You can call someone from the jail."

Minnie changed from a charging bull into a whimpering child. "But he's in there and he's all alone."

Greta felt sorry for the woman. She truly did. But

there was no way she was letting her inside the house after Kyle said no.

Greta helped Minnie into the backseat of the club cab truck. With a click, Kyle locked the doors then pushed the button to keep them that way. He turned on the radio and listened to the Sulphur High School football game as he drove back to the police station. The commentators were all excited about the game and kept calling it the Murray County Bowl. From what Greta could ascertain, the Sulphur Bulldogs were playing the Davis Wolves and they were staunch rivals. Whoever won the game held important bragging rights for the next year.

"You made me miss this game," Kyle told Henry.

"You think I care," the old man snarled.

Quickly, the truck filled with the smell of cheap whiskey. Greta was thankful the station wasn't six or seven miles away but only a few blocks. She could see the lights of the football field and when Kyle parked the truck and opened the doors, she could hear the roar of the crowd and the voices of the sportscasters coming through the speakers.

Kyle sat them across the room from each other and read them each their rights. "Okay, you two, you're staying right here until you sober up and cool down."

"What about my cat? You said I could make a phone call," Minnie whined.

"I'm calling first. You arrested me first so I get to make the call. She's not about to call her fat old sister to come take care of Riggs. Woman will feed him ice cream and kill him dead." Henry slurred his words.

"My sister is not fat!" Minnie yelled. "And I'm calling her to take care of Riggs. You'd just call your brother and he don't have the sense of a half-dead gnat. He'd let Riggs out on the road and get him killed quicker than Mary givin' him ice cream. You know he likes a little ice cream on Friday nights while we listen to the ball game."

Henry glared at her. "You done cheated me out of that too. Put me in a cell, Kyle. I'm tar'd to death of lookin' at this woman. Can I have a radio or can you at least turn up the one in the 'patcher's office so I don't miss the last half of the game? Dratted woman. I wish she'd divorce me. My head hurts. Can I have an aspirin?"

Minnie pointed a shaky finger at Greta and then at Henry. "Find me a cell far away from him as possible and I demand that I get to use the phone right now."

"Can't make a phone call until I finish the paperwork," Kyle said. "Greta, don't you let her near the phone. You both can sit in a cell and think about the way you've acted. When I get my work done we'll talk about making those phone calls."

Minnie set her jaw and Henry mumbled all the way back to the cell block. In a few minutes, Kyle returned and took Minnie to her cell. She cussed, ranted, raved, called him everything except a white policeman, and threatened to call PETA instead of her sister. Why, she'd have KTEN News on the front lawn of the police station by daylight and Kyle wasn't going to have a job or a set of handcuffs.

"Why would she call PETA? You didn't do anything to harm her cat did you?" Greta asked when Kyle returned and sat down behind a computer to fill in the forms for his arrest.

"Oh, she's just had too much whiskey. Come morning they'll both be sorry for the way they've acted."

"You going to be long?" she asked.

"It'll take a little while."

"Then I'm going to my computer to work too. Come on back and get me when you're ready to go."

"I'm sorry. I could take you on home. Are you working for Jodie tonight?"

"No, I'm just reading a good book. Jodie's singing out at the ballroom and Etta's gone off on another excursion with Roxie. We don't have guests this week. Not until Sunday. Etta and Roxie are regular old gadabouts these days. Just holler when you get finished," she said.

He nodded and turned on the radio sitting on his desk. Score was tied. Sulphur swept in from five yards out for their second touchdown, bringing the score to 13–7. They missed the point after and a list of new team members taking the field was given. The kick was high and good, giving the Bulldogs time to run downfield toward the Davis Wolves. The blockers did their job and created a hole so big the catcher floated right through it and ran the ball back for a touchdown. Score tied again, only Davis pulled a fake punt and ran the ball in for the extra points, giving them a lead of two points. Kyle gritted his teeth. He'd looked forward to this game all week and had ten dollars riding on Sulphur winning.

Greta typed in witness reports and dates, flipping page after page in the folder she'd been working on most of the afternoon. She might finish it by Tuesday if Wilma didn't need help with the new programs concerning payroll and arrest reports. Before long, it wouldn't take Kyle so long to get his reports done. Not when Greta had given him and the other nine men on the force a two-hour lesson in the new way of doing things. That ought to scald the hair right out of his little ears, for her to be the teacher and him the student. But Wilma had already approached the council and they'd agreed to let Greta teach them the basics about the programs to make their jobs easier.

She was so engrossed in the report from back in the late fifties that she was processing that she didn't hear Kyle tap on the door frame of her small office. He cleared his throat and she jumped.

"Didn't mean to startle you," he said.

"Well, you did. For a minute there I had a vision of Minnie with that knife again. You think she would have really split his head open?"

"No doubt about it. They get liquored up and go at each other about every six months. Usually it's closer to midnight and I don't have to take the call. I should have gotten home quicker or turned off my radio and I would have avoided it tonight."

She pushed buttons on her computer. A few bars of music sounded and the screen went dark. "Why every six months?"

"That's how long it takes to brew a fight in their world, I suppose. She accuses him of cheating."

Greta was stunned. "Who in their right mind would cheat with him?"

"Good point, but when cheap whiskey is talking, it doesn't have a lot of common sense. He accuses her of turning Riggs against him. Usually we can just talk to them and they end up forgiving the other one and hugging old Riggs between them."

"But tonight they got out the kitchen hardware," she said.

"Yes, they did. Minnie's already calling down the empty cells to him that she's sorry and loves him, and he's calling her sweetheart. By morning, they'll be fine."

"They won't be going to trial?" Greta asked. "You mean I risked getting cut open for them and . . . of course, neither of them will press charges on the other one. I wouldn't have your job for all the dirt in Texas. And I'm coming to believe that most marriages are not made in heaven, either."

"You got that right," he said.

"You said you'd never been married so what makes you an authority?"

"I've never been married but I'm as much an authority as you, Miss Fields," he said shortly.

"I bet old Henry was just like you when he was young. Minnie married him thinking he'd change, but guess what? No such luck!"

"And Minnie was probably just like you. Wanted her way all the time and fussed and fumed until she got it."

"You are rotten to the core."

"And you are an angel," he said sarcastically.

She stood up and pushed her chair in. "I'm ready to go home. Is the ball game over?"

"It's over. Sulphur lost its two-year reign. Davis won by two points and I lost ten dollars."

"Oh, how pitiful. You poor baby."

"Don't tease about something as big as the Murray County Bowl. This is small-town America. Football is a very big thing." He continued to block the door. She was scarcely two feet from him, apparently ready to go home, but he wasn't ready to take her. He didn't like the feelings barreling through him like an Angus bull in a gift shop. One kiss. Just one and he'd see quickly that she held no sway over him, that she was a shrew just like Minnie on the nights when the old girl had half a bottle of Jim Beam in her.

She expected him to step back when she started out the door. When he didn't she ran right into his chest. He looked down and she looked up. Electricity filled the air. He ran his knuckles down the smooth plane of her jawbone. Tingles did a fast two-step up and down her arms. His eyes were all dreamy and half open and she didn't want him to kiss her. Better to not know than know beyond a doubt and not be able to do a thing about it. She absolutely refused to fall for Kyle Parsons. Not even if he promised to move to Paris—France, not Texas—with her and said he owned an oil well that produced a million dollars a year in revenue.

"Thanks for letting me get my work done," he whispered.

"No problem," she said.

He bent somewhat, and she got up on tiptoes ever so slightly. Their lips met in the middle. He wrapped his arms around her, pulling her tight against his chest. Her heart kept fast time with his. He wished that she could be anyone else in the world but Roseanna's sister-in-law. Anyone but Greta Fields, the rich girl from Tulsa, who'd never be satisfied in Sulphur, Oklahoma, with a common old rancher-slash-policeman.

Static from the radio caused Kyle to step back as if the dispatcher could hear what had just happened. "You still in the building, Kyle?"

He pushed the button and turned his head. "I'm still here but I've clocked out. I'm going home."

"Game's over. Folks is going home and there don't seem to be any ruckus over the winners or losers so the night crew can handle the crowd. Got a lady in here to see you."

Greta picked up her purse and tried to ignore the voice.

A prickly heat began on Kyle's neck. "Who?"

"Says she's your wife."

"LaNita?" Kyle gasped.

A sweet, silky smooth southern voice replaced the dispatchers. "That's right, darlin'. I've come home to spend a night or two."

Greta wiped the back of her hand across her mouth and stormed past him, down the hall, and into the office.

Wordlessly, he followed her. Dang it anyway. He didn't owe her an explanation even though his mind kept trying to form words to tell her about LaNita.

"Darlin'!" The tall lady crossed the room in three easy strides and wrapped her arms around his neck, kissed him on the cheek, and leaned back to study his physique from eyebrows to toenails.

While she gave Kyle a thorough once-over, Greta did the same to her. Taller than Roseanna with legs even longer, she stood eye to eye with Kyle and he had to be at least six foot three. Her skin was permanently tanned, a soft coffee with lots of pure cream. Her cheekbones high and twinkling eyes so dark they were almost black. Her outfit smacked of money and the shoes practically had Greta swooning. It was her hair that gave away that she was part African American. Thick soft curls framed her delicate face. LaNita? Where had Greta heard that name?

Then she remembered. LaNita Washburn. The super-model. New York City. Two years ago when she and her mother attended the fashion show. LaNita modeled for

Versace. At the last showing, she wore a white negligee and swept down the runway on satin bedroom slippers that had four-inch spike heels.

LaNita was Kyle Parsons' wife?

"I'm home, darlin'. Are you glad to see me?" she crooned.

"Of course, I'm always glad to see you. Why haven't you called?"

"Because I've been busy. I'm on my way from New York to Houston. Decided to make it a road trip instead of flying. I want a whole night to do nothing but sleep, then tomorrow night we'll go to supper and play catch-up. I'll have to leave Sunday morning. They start the shoot in Houston on Monday morning and I can't have bags under my eyes."

"Sounds like a plan to me," Kyle said.

The man was certifiably goofy. The men in the white jackets from the insane asylum would come cart him off with that ludicrous grin spreading across his face. Crazy and a liar to boot. Twice Greta had asked him if he'd ever been married and both times he denied it, and yet there stood living proof.

"Good, then I'll follow you home. My Lamborghini is outside in a NO PARKING slot so I suppose we'd better get going," she said.

As if lightning struck, he stuttered when he looked at Greta. "I've got to take this woman home. She's working off some community service time for driving too fast."

"Well, hurry, darlin'. I might be able to keep my eyes

open for a little bit of conversation. Is there any wine in the house?"

"Not a bit. There's Coke and Dr Pepper and a pitcher of sweet tea, but no wine," he said.

She laughed. "Then tea it is."

"You still got a key?" he asked.

She raised an eyebrow and blew him a kiss as she left. "Yes, I do. See you at home in a few minutes?"

"If that don't beat all," the dispatcher said. "I figured she'd had enough of Sulphur when she left out of here the last time."

"She'll get her fill and be gone for another two or three years," Kyle said. "You ready, Greta?"

She didn't even give him a nod but plowed outside, let herself in the pickup, and fumed. He'd tilted her world with a kiss, an adulterous one at that. She'd never trust him again. She'd get through the sentence and go home to a world that made sense.

He slid into the driver's seat and started up the engine. "Guess I'd better explain."

"Why?"

He made a left turn, driving slowly. "Because this is not what it looks like."

"And just what is it? You're married to LaNita Washburn who is a supermodel. Right?"

"No, not right. It's a joke between us. We're not married, not really."

"How can you be married but not really? Either you are or you are not," she said.

"It's a long story. I started to tell you the other night. She called and said if she had time she'd come by for a couple of days. Sometimes I don't hear from her for months and months then she'll show up on my doorstep. If she's got a long layover in Oklahoma City or Dallas, she'll rent a car and come around for a visit every few years. She loves to drive, says it's the best nerve medicine in the world. She's stayed as little as an hour or as long as a week. My place is a refuge none of her friends know anything about."

"Sounds like no one knows about your marriage either," Greta smarted off, her heart still stinging from the betrayal.

"God, I hope not. The tabloids would have a heyday with that news."

"The self-righteous Mr. Parsons takes the Lord's name in vain. Think that or your adulterous heart will keep you out of heaven?"

"Are you jealous?"

"Me? Hell, no!"

"Then what do you care if I'm married or not? Mercy, all we shared was a little kiss that meant nothing. It was just a passing fancy."

Her heart dropped through the floorboard and bounced along the rough highway.

"The story goes like this. LaNita spent a lot of time in Tatums. It was an all-black town when it was first settled. Her mother is a lovely black lady lawyer who works in Norman, and her father is a white businessman. She actually grew up in Norman but her grand-mother lived in Tatums and she spent summers there. I didn't know her back in those days. We met at college. She was going to be a schoolteacher but got 'discov-ered.' " He turned loose of the steering wheel and made quotation marks in the air. "That ended her teaching ambitions and sent her off to New York City."

"And you were already married? Why didn't you get a divorce?"

"Didn't need to get one."

One look at her face said she was furious.

"Well, short story is we never got married. We're just such good friends that we act like an old married cou-ple and people got to teasing us about being married and she finally told them we were actually married and . . ." He stopped to suck up another lungful of air; nothing was coming out right. "Never did even date, not really. She comes home for a visit and it's a big joke when she calls herself my wife. It's a joke, honest. We've always been best friends ever since college and we wouldn't ruin that for any kind of romance."

"Yeah, right. And what was that about oceanfront property in the middle of the Sahara? You two eloped and never divorced and now if you did the tabloids would get hold of it and end of story," Greta said.

He pulled up in the driveway and turned to face Greta. "We did not elope and we are not married. It's the truth. She'll probably be asleep when I get home and won't wake up all day tomorrow. We'll go to Davis for supper tomorrow night because she loves Mexican food and there's a place on Main Street over there. Las Cascadas. She'll eat her way through a couple of plates of enchiladas and three or four sopapillas and we'll talk until midnight. Then she'll be gone. . . . Oh, why am I trying to make you understand any of this anyway? It's none of your business."

"You got that right. Don't bother walking me to the door. I'm sure you are in a hurry to get home to your wife."

"You bet I am." He gritted his teeth.

She slammed the door so hard it shook the whole truck.

He slapped the steering wheel and slung gravel when he backed out. Dang woman anyway. He'd be glad when she went back to her precious big city.

Chapter Nine

A fall nip was in the air that Sunday morning promising that summer would not last forever. Soft rain had fallen most of the night and clouds still hung low in the sky. The weather fit right in with Greta's dark mood. She'd worked from daylight to dark the previous day in the yard. Trey taught her how to start the push mower and the weed eater. When she'd finished those jobs, she pruned the roses and cleaned the flower beds. She didn't enjoy the work but it kept her hands busy even if it didn't stop visions of LaNita on that runway platform in New York. By bedtime Etta was singing her praises, but all the compliments couldn't lift the heavy mood from the night before.

It had to do with Kyle and that so-called fake wife of his. Greta had researched the information on her laptop computer after Kyle brought her home the night before. Was he was telling her the truth and there wasn't a legal marriage with LaNita?

"Why do you even care?" she said aloud as she got dressed.

She sat with Rosy and Trey in church. Rosy wore a lovely light green sheath dress with gold buttons up the front and shoes only a shade darker. Trey looked his usual handsome self in a black Italian suit, tailored a couple of years ago since the lapels were a bit wider this year. Not that anyone in Sulphur would notice the difference, but Greta did. Trey held Rosy's hand and whispered in her ear a few times. Greta's heart longed for a man to treat her like that. Rich. Poor. Who cared if his lapels were slightly out-of-date? What Wilma said suddenly made sense. Trey wasn't going to get tired of Rosy this time. He was in Sulphur because he wanted to be, because he was happy.

The preacher read from 1 Corinthians 13 about love. He said that love was long suffering and went on to give examples. Greta didn't hear him but thought about Kyle. Did he secretly hope someday that LaNita would come home to roost for good and then they could go to the courthouse and really get married? She shook her head and caught the end of a sentence about love never failing.

Yeah, right! It failed Trey and Rosy on the first try and evidently it failed Stella and Rance as well as Dee.

Oh, no it did not, her conscience said. *Love didn't*

fail. It was lack of love and commitment on one or both sides that failed.

A silent argument waged while the preacher went on with his sermon. In this corner in her only good Sunday dress, the red one she'd worn to Trey and Rosy's reception, was Greta, arguing that love wasn't all perfect like the preacher advocated. In the other corner was her conscience, decked out in robes of righteousness, and arguing with a vengeance that true love was pure, lasting, and perfect.

The debate went on until the preacher announced that at two o'clock that afternoon there would be a senior citizens' ice cream social in the fellowship hall. Kyle Parsons' youth group would crank the ice cream and serve it to all those fifty-five and older. He winked broadly and said that no one would be asking for identification at the door so anyone who felt like a senior citizen would be welcome.

After the last "Amen" and the sanctuary was finally empty, ten junior high kids, Greta, and Kyle met in the kitchen to make brownies and ice cream. Kyle and the boys brought in three ice cream freezers. Greta and the girls put on bibbed aprons they found hanging on a hook behind the kitchen door and dragged out pans to make brownies and sugar cookies. Mixes for both, but hopefully the older ladies wouldn't be too quick to judge a bunch of teenaged girls and one woman who'd just begun to learn the complicated art of reading a recipe.

Greta pulled her hair back into a ponytail at the nape of her neck and kicked her shoes off. "Okay, ladies, let's get this show on the road. I figure we'll do the brownies first. Two nine-by-twelve cake pans will fit in the oven at one time. We can do four batches in an hour. So Kelsey, you and Molly mix the first two boxes, and Molly, Cathy, and Sueann can get the pans greased and ready. I checked this morning when I brought in the supplies. They make four pans, so if we work as a team, it'll go faster. While the brownies are cooking, then you can get the cookie dough made and ready to cook."

"Greta, is this the way it's supposed to look? It's pretty stiff. Did we forget to put something in the mix?" Kelsey called her over to look. She had followed Greta's example and pulled her dishwater-blond hair back with a rubber band. Strands of it escaped immediately to hang in her eyes.

"Greta, is this enough butter in the pans?" Amber needed reassurance that she and her team were doing their job properly.

Kyle used the phone in the kitchen to order pizzas for lunch. "Yes, eight large pizzas. Two pepperoni. One cheese. Two hamburger. Two supreme, and one that's half black olive and half Canadian bacon. That would be great. We're in the kitchen at the Baptist church."

"Eight?" Greta said.

"Five growing boys. Want to bet we don't have a slice left at two o'clock? Five dollars? You buy supper tomorrow night after work?" Kyle asked.

"I'm not betting in a church. The brownies would burn or the ice cream wouldn't set up. What are you thinking about? You've been standing too close to your make-believe wife all weekend." Greta answered.

"Shhhh." He laid a finger across her lips.

His touch affected her in a way she didn't like one bit.

"Don't say things like that so loud. They'll ask a million questions. And she's not my wife. We aren't married. It was just a joke that got out of hand."

"So you say."

Jim called from the other side of the kitchen. "Hey, Kyle, is it our turn to churn? They've had their fifteen minutes haven't they?"

Kyle checked his watch. "Yes it is. Pizza will be here in twenty minutes. Is that your stomach growling, Andy?"

"It sure is. I'm starving plumb to death. I could eat half an Angus bull. Just chop off the horns, slap him on the grill for two minutes, and put 'im on my plate." The boy was so skinny it didn't look like he could finish a Happy Meal much less half a steer. Someday when he grew into all those elbows and knees and other knobby bones, he might be a big man. He was tall enough, but a good gust of wind could blow him all the way to Texas.

Kyle turned back to Greta. "So you think I've overordered? Bet on or off?"

"Definitely off. I'm not dodging lightning bolts."

She made a face at him and went back to her corner of the room where the girls had begun to place the cookies in even rows on the pans. So he was still touchy about LaNita? Just what had gone on between them back in their college days? Had they been more than friends? Did more happen?

It began to rain in earnest, beating against the window above the sink. The boys kept turning the freezer.

The electricity blinked.

Greta was glad they were using manual freezers instead of electric ones.

The girls squealed. The boys laughed.

Greta moaned.

"See just what happens when you talk about a bet in church! What happens if it blows the electricity? Half-cooked brownies. Raw cookies. See what you did?" she yelled across the room.

"What's she talking about?" Jim asked.

"She's got a burr under her saddle. Women get like that," Kyle said.

"You better watch out over there," Sueann piped up. "We'll all gang up on you and you know if we do you ain't got a chance." She was the shortest one of the five and had the best figure, coming into a mature beauty ahead of her friends. She had shoulder-length, medium brown hair worn parted in the middle and straight, piercing gray eyes the color of fog, and a clear complexion.

Greta smiled. Even if it was five girls who were barely teenagers, she had a few friends in Sulphur, Oklahoma.

At fifteen minutes until the party was to begin, she had brownies cut and arranged on a big glass platter and sugar cookies complete with icing and sprinkles on another. She had a dab of icing on her cheek and her apron sported streaks of brownie batter and butter. Kyle thought she was lovelier than she had been at the wedding reception all those weeks ago.

He had to give her credit where it was due. From the time the judge had given her five minutes to make a choice between jail and going home with Etta, she'd taken her medicine like an adult instead of a spoiled little girl. She hadn't whined and whimpered but did exactly what she was told.

Dogs and kids. You couldn't fool either. His dogs took to her. And all five girls in the youth group loved her. So why couldn't the two of them spend five minutes in each other's presence without fighting? An anomaly for sure!

He'd figured she'd be late every day when he went to pick her up but she was ready. She'd already reorganized Wilma's computer and the woman couldn't sing her praises loud enough. Who would have ever thought such a thing could happen? Certainly not Kyle or anyone else in the station house. Wilma ran things with a tough hand and hated all new things. Greta had swept in, barely more than a convict, and Wilma had been open to her suggestions.

Greta turned to find him staring. "What are you looking at?"

"Are you going to wear that apron to the social?"

"I might, and I might go barefoot too. You got a problem with that? Tell me, why are we doing this anyway?

Is there an agenda for the youth group or is it just something you pop out of your head? Or are you planning things just to make me mad?"

Kyle was glad the kids were setting up the dining room in preparation for the social. Some of them came from broken homes where he was sure they endured too much arguing and fighting. He sure didn't want that atmosphere within the youth group. "I don't care if you go in there with icing on your chin or flour on your nose, Greta. It makes me . . . no, never mind. The reason we're doing this is because I plan one activity each month for the youth group. This one is to teach them to be considerate to their elders. To listen to their stories. To help them. To respect them. I couldn't care less if it makes you mad or glad, lady."

"And what is on the agenda for next month? Oh, I'm probably not allowed to be privy to that information since I'm just here as a community service convict," she said.

He gritted his teeth. She'd been a prophet when she said Roseanna Cahill was a kitten compared to her. A man would be crazy to fall for the woman. He'd been an idiot to ever have kissed her. "On the first weekend in October, which is two weeks from yesterday, we will paint Miss Iris' house. She's ninety years old and still lives alone over on Oklahoma Street in a small two-bedroom house. That will teach them to be considerate and helpful, and it will help Miss Iris who lives on a fixed income and couldn't afford to pay someone to do the work. If the weather permits, we'll paint it for her that day and have a sack lunch on the lawn."

"And if the weather doesn't permit?"

"We'll cross that bridge when we get to it," he said.

It was on the tip of her tongue to make a comment about the weather when the early birds arrived at ten minutes before the hour. She peeled off the apron and used the mirror on the back of the kitchen door to clean icing from her face. Her shoes felt tight when she slipped her feet back into them but she wouldn't give him the satisfaction of saying a word. She put on her best smile and went to greet the elderly folks and help where she was needed.

Etta patted an empty chair beside her. "Good brownies."

Greta sat for a moment, glad to be off her feet. In the month she'd been in Murray County, she'd worked in sneakers and worn work boots to the barns. Used to be that she could wear high heels all day and then dance in them half the night. Was this place beginning to ooze its redneck ways into her life? Now that was a terrifying thought.

"The girls did a good job. They work well together," Greta said.

"Why don't you invite them all to the lodge one Saturday night for makeovers? I've got tons of old makeup and nail polish and I'm sure Jodie and Rosy could donate even more. Kyle could take the boys out on a camping trip or some such thing. You and the girls could have a slumber party. Make cookies. Whatever you do at those things." Etta spooned ice cream into her mouth between sentences.

"If it's a weekend when Etta's got guests you can bring them down to my place," Roxie said from across the table.

"Jodie has makeup?" Greta couldn't get past that one sentence.

"Yes, she cleans up really good when it's necessary. You saw her at the Arbuckle Ballroom. Didn't you realize she was wearing makeup then? Now don't go getting any visions of her looking like me. They don't make that much makeup in the world." Roxie smiled. It was hard to think of her being past sixty but she had to be that old at least. Tally was in her thirties so that would make her mother at least fifty, so Roxie might even be looking seventy in the eye. With her ratted red hair, bright pink ruffled dress, and matching shoes, she looked more like Shirley MacLaine playing a part in a movie than a bed-and-breakfast madam in Sulphur, Oklahoma.

Greta laughed with her. "Etta, that sounds like a fine idea. I'll ask the girls and maybe we'll do that for our weekend in November. It'll be too cold to go swimming or have an outdoor activity."

"Just check the calendar to be sure we don't have guests that weekend. I've noticed Kelsey is starting to wear makeup and some Sundays she looks like she's put on eye shadow with a putty knife. You could sure help them and they'd think it was a fun night," Etta said.

Greta leaned forward and hugged the woman. "Thank you."

The last of the stragglers left the party at four o'clock. By four-thirty they had the kitchen put to rights, the fellowship hall straightened, and had discussed the upcoming paint job on Miss Iris Smith's house. They'd each bring a sack lunch. Kyle would provide a cooler full of soft drinks and afterward they'd all go back to his trailer for a movie and hamburgers.

"And what's happening in November?" Kelsey asked.

"Maybe you girls could come to the lodge and we'll have a slumber party," Greta said. "The guys could do something with Kyle and . . ."

"Won't work," Kyle shook his head. "The last weekend of October is going to be our November activity. You'll all be busy during November with Thanksgiving and family things. I'm planning a trip to Oklahoma City the first two days of your fall school break. Overnighter in a motel."

"That's outside Murray County. You'd better talk Jodie or someone else into going as a sponsor for the girls," Greta said.

"Okay." Kyle agreed much too readily to suit her. "You kids will need to talk to your parents about it. We'll take the church van and we'll need for them to sign permission forms for the trip. In December we'll have our Christmas party out at my house. I think the ice cream social was a success. You all worked hard and I'm proud of you. We might do another one in February.

Maybe a Valentine's theme. Okay, load up in the van and I'll take you all home."

Not a thank you for her idea or all the hard work she'd put in all afternoon. Nary a word about her taking some initiative and trying to do something with the girls on her own. Just a shake of the head and kablooey, there went her plans all blown to bits like a balloon when a kid pokes it with a pin. She pulled the seat belt across her chest and stared out the window. He kept a running conversation going with first one and then another and didn't even speak to her until he had them all delivered.

He stopped in front of the lodge and turned to look at her. "What are you pouting about?"

"I do not pout."

"Yes, you do, and you've been doing it ever since I said the activity in November was a trip to Oklahoma City. If you want to have a slumber party with the girls, by all means have one. It doesn't have to be their activity for the month, Greta. It can just be you being nice enough to have them over for a slumber party. I don't have to do anything with the boys that weekend," he said.

"What do you do when you take them to Oklahoma City?" she asked.

"They only go to school three days that week. Fall break is scheduled. So we leave on Thursday morning, go to Omniplex for two or three hours, eat lunch at the Spaghetti Warehouse, then check in to a motel with an indoor pool, and let them play until bedtime. The next day we take advantage of the free breakfast bar at the hotel. After we check out we do the Bass Pro Shop for a couple of hours. The girls whine but it teaches them patience. Then we have lunch and drive to Norman where the girls can do the mall for a couple of hours. The boys whine but it teaches them patience. We get home before supper on Friday. That way if their parents have plans with them for the weekend, they are free. And besides, that's the night of the Sulphur Halloween carnival so it'll leave them free for it if they want to go."

"I see," she said.

"I'm sure if Jodie isn't tied up she'll go along with us. I'll just have to ask her. If she is, there are a few other women in the church who've stepped in and helped me in the past. You don't have to go. Come on, I'll walk you to the door and then I've got to hurry through chores before Sunday night services."

"I don't need you to hold my hand. I'm a big girl. I can walk myself to the door. Oh, which reminds me, did LaNita have a nice time?"

"LaNita is still there. She got word that her photo shoot has been postponed until Tuesday. It's an outside, on-the-beach thing and it's raining in Galveston tomorrow. Supposed to be sunny on Tuesday though. She's leaving tomorrow morning. Why? Jealous?"

"Of course not," she said with a flip of her hair as she got out of the van.

Chapter Ten

The guests at the lodge gathered in the dining room and sipped coffee until Rosy and Greta filled the sideboard with breakfast. Steaming hot biscuits in a basket covered with red and white checks. A crockpot full of sausage gravy. Oven omelets. An assortment of Etta's homemade jellies and jams.

The oldest man in the group was first in line. "Now this is real breakfast. The kind I was raised on."

Nine people filed in behind him. They had arrived Friday night and were booked at the lodge until Monday morning. The youngest of the group was well past seventy, the oldest pushing ninety.

"Which one of you ladies made these eggs? Would you be willin' to move to Louisiana and be my personal chef?" the older one, Chet, asked.

Rosy circled the table refilling coffee cups. Breakfast was served buffet style but she always played the hostess. "Greta made the eggs this morning."

"I'll pay twice what Chet offers you and I'll live longer so your job won't be cut short. How about it?" Albert teased.

Sally, Albert's wife, poked him in the arm with her fork. "You old coot. You might get away with eating like this for a weekend. But any longer than that and your cholesterol would cause you to drop dead of a heart attack."

"Ah, but what a way to die." Albert sighed.

"If you clean up your plates, Greta's bringing out a pan of iced, warm cinnamon rolls in a minute," Rosy said.

Chet groaned. "Momma, will you bring me to live here when I get old?"

His wife, Dolly, grinned. "Honey, I hate to tell you this, but you're already old."

Greta loved the good-natured bantering among the five couples. They were attending a huge family reunion over in Davis at somewhere called Deer Creek Lodge. Chet had told them at supper the previous night that all those children and video games drove the old folks up the wall the year before so they'd made up their minds to visit the reunion during the day but to stay elsewhere.

Chet held up his coffee to be filled. "Sure beats cold cereal or doughnuts over at the reunion."

"You act surprised today when they bring in that

cake and start singing. I know Skyler let the cat out of the bag yesterday but they've gone to a lot of trouble," Dolly said.

"I'm old, not stupid. I'd have to listen to you nag at me for another seventy years if I didn't act surprised," Chet said.

"We've been married seventy years today," Dolly explained. "They're doing this big surprise thing and the seven-year-old great-great-granddaughter told Chet all about the cake yesterday while they were fishing."

Greta set a pan of warm cinnamon rolls in the middle of the table. "Congratulations. What's your secret?" If she found someone and got married within the next six months she'd be ninety-five by the time she was married seventy years. She couldn't begin to fathom such a thing.

"Secret is we got married when we were sixteen and eighteen and grew up together. Had some rough times and some not so rough but we stuck it out," Chet said.

"Secret is to let him think he's boss." Dolly winked.

"I am the boss," Chet protested.

"See how well it works," Dolly whispered behind her hand.

Greta was still smiling when Kyle rapped on the door. She wore her oldest pair of hand-me-down jeans, a faded T-shirt with a hole in the sleeve, and had pulled her hair back in a ponytail at the nape of her neck. He said they'd be outside painting most of the day so she didn't bother with makeup. Lately she did that more and more. In her pre-kill-the-bull wreck days, she wouldn't have gone outside to pick up the morning paper without makeup.

"Sorry I'm a few minutes late. LaNita called early this morning and we had a long visit over the phone. She's in Rome this week doing a photo shoot for Versace's new line, and then I had chores to do."

The smile vanished.

"Anyway, I've already delivered the kids to Miss Iris' house and they're mowing and running the weed eater."

"I thought we were painting," she said coldly.

"We are but the yard needed one more mowing and we had to get the weeds from the base of the house to be able to paint. They should have the job done by the time we get there. It's a small yard but Miss Iris isn't able for much these days. I did smell peanut butter cookies when she stuck her head out the back door and said she'd have cookies and Kool-Aid for break time in the middle of the morning."

As they drove through the park, she noticed a few yellow and orange leaves among the lush green foliage. The aroma of sulfur water hung in the air like rotten eggs, but she'd grown used to it. But she determined that was the extent of what she'd get used to in Sulphur. In another eight weeks she could get back to her life as she knew it, and it wouldn't be a day too soon. LaNita phoned and they'd had a visit, did they? And she was much more important than ten kids with a house to paint.

You are jealous, her conscience singsonged.

I am not, she argued silently.

Yes, you are, and that means you care about Kyle. The voice in her head wouldn't be hushed and kept repeating the phrase over and over until he parked in the driveway of a very small white frame house on Oklahoma Street.

"Here we are. Looks like they're geared up and ready to work," Kyle said.

All five girls came running to the truck to open the door and literally hauled her out by the arms to come to their side of the house. They had a bet running with the boys that they could paint their half faster than the guys could theirs.

"And what's the bet involve?" Greta asked.

"An extra hour," Cathy said seriously. "If we win, they only get one hour at the Bass Pro Shop." She snarled her nose. "If they do, we only get one hour at the mall and they get three at fishing heaven."

Greta grimaced. She wouldn't even be going on that trip, but she'd work until she dropped to see Kyle have to spend three hours in the mall. Maybe he would spend his three hours looking at poster-sized prints of LaNita in the clothing stores. "Well, where's the paint? Let's show the guys that we're tougher than they are," she said.

They led her to the back of the house where paint cans were already open and ready. Jim, Andy, Kade, Jason, and Kenny stood ready with paintbrushes in hand at the west end of the house.

"Don't you be putting one drop of paint on this house until Kyle says go, or you'll be disqualified and we won't have to go the mall at all," Andy said.

"Okay, ladies, you can pick up your brushes," Kyle said.

So who died and made him God? Did he always get to run the show?

Greta picked up a brush.

"Not you, Greta. This is their project. You and I are the judges, not the contestants. We will watch our groups to see that they don't miss a spot or have runs in the paint. The job must be done well or they don't get credit. Now, on your mark, get set, dip the brushes and . . ." He paused then yelled, "Go!"

The boys took off like lightning, painting in a group tumbling all over one another and claiming this spot or that one. The girls had organized their places, pouring paint in smaller coffee cans they'd brought from home so each of them had paint in one hand and a brush in the other. Sueann took over painting the bottom three wide siding boards. They gave her time to get three feet ahead and then Cathy began the next six boards. When she'd painted a section, Amber stretched up to reach the next four boards. By then Molly had a ladder propped up and followed behind her. Kelsey brought up the rear, brushing paint on the eaves. In less than an hour, the girls reached the end of the longer north side and started the east end. When Sueann finished, she kept going right on around the front of the house, which faced the south. The boys had completed the west end and were finally turning the corner, only to find the girls already done with their portion and helping to finish theirs. They all met at the front porch, the girls high-fiving each other and the boys moaning.

"Girls win," Greta announced. "Not a drop of paint on any of the windows. No runs and not a one of them looks like you boys. Y'all look like you took a bath in the paint."

"Oh, we paint faster because we thought about it all night and figured out a way to not get in each other's way," Kelsey said. "Those boys paint three coats at once: the house, the ground, and themselves."

"Come on. Call off the bet," Kade begged. "We can't see hardly nothing in just an hour at the Pro Shop."

Sueann shook her head. "No way. We need that extra hour at the mall. Y'all can play video games or sit outside the stores and pout. Now, if you want another try at winning, we can bet you we can clean our brushes faster than you. If you win, you get your hour back. If we win, we don't go to the fishing store at all."

"I wouldn't place a bet like that for nothin'," Jim shuddered.

Miss Iris opened the front door. "Cookies and Kool-Aid coming right out."

Greta rushed to help her with the platter. Kelsey followed suit and brought out the pitcher of red Kool-Aid.

Greta had expected a withered-up old woman who looked like one of those folk dolls made from dried apples. Miss Iris was just over five feet tall with a ramrod straight back and few wrinkles in her face. She was as round as she was tall and had only a few streaks of silver in her jet-black hair. She sat down in a white rocking chair with wide arms and watched the kids devour a whole plate of cookies and two pitchers of Kool-Aid.

"And you're the new lady in town who's helping Kyle with this bunch." Miss Iris eyed Greta seriously. "You like it here?"

"No, ma'am, I do not. I've always lived in the city and right after Thanksgiving I'm going back there," Greta answered honestly.

"Why are you staying until Thanksgiving? Looks to me if you don't like it you'd leave soon as you could," Iris said.

"That is, as soon as I *can*. I'm under orders to stay until then. I had a wreck and—"

"Oh, I heard about that. Killed Kyle's bull and now you have to work with him. Wilma says she wishes you'd have another wreck and kill another bull when you drive out of town so she could keep you a while longer. She's my niece, Wilma is. She says you were sent from heaven to help her get through these next few months. Retiring, she is. The last day of December is her last day at the station. Going to start off the New Year right with no job."

Greta picked up another cookie. "Do you give out your recipes? These are wonderful."

"Sure I do. But the recipe ain't the secret to good cookies. It's watching them close and cooking them the full time. Way I figure it is, cake is soft, cookies is crisp."

Greta nodded.

"Now tell me about you and Kyle," Iris whispered.

The kids and Kyle had taken the paintbrushes to the backyard to clean them up under the water faucet sticking up three feet and located right under a big pecan tree.

Greta rolled her eyes toward the blue sky. Why did everyone in this town think there was something between her and Kyle Parsons? Just because she'd been thrown into his company didn't mean she wanted to be there or that she wouldn't run from it as soon as it was legally possible. "There is no me and Kyle. He's got a girlfriend, LaNita."

"Oh, that's not his girlfriend. That girl is just his friend. Met her in college and she comes around sometimes. She was here last month for the first time in years. Now, Roseanna was his girlfriend. Let's see, Roseanna is your sister-in-law, now, ain't she? Well, she stepped out with him before she met your brother. We all knew that wouldn't work. They'd clash worse than oil and water. Rosy has that Cahill temper and Kyle is as hardheaded as a bull."

"Who else has he dated?" Greta asked.

"Oh, there was that girl from Davis. She was a schoolteacher over there but we knew that was a passing fancy too. She did everything he wanted and took his supper all cooked and ready out to his house most every night. Lasted about a month. Kyle got tired of all that smotherin' right quick."

"So he's an anomaly," Greta said.

Iris' eyes glittered. "Yes, he is. Thought I'd be so old I wouldn't know that word, didn't you? I'm an old dinosaur schoolteacher. Taught until I was seventy years old and they had to run me out of the classroom. But you are right. He wants to be the boss but he doesn't want to feel like he's lost his holy rights as the man of the house. It'll take a special woman to bring him to the altar."

"Whoever she is, she has my sympathy," Greta said at the same time the kids all came back from the yard.

"Well, didn't take as long as you all figured, did it?" Iris quickly changed the subject.

"No, guess we'll take our sack lunches to the park and take a hike before I haul this rowdy bunch out to my house for the afternoon," Kyle said.

"Well, I do thank the bunch of you for a wonderful job," Iris said.

"You are very welcome," the kids singsonged in harmony.

"Come with us to the park, Miss Iris," Kelsey said.

"Oh, no, not me. Thanks for the invite but my favorite cartoons are coming on in five minutes. Y'all run along and have a good time. Me, I'm going to sit in my recliner and enjoy the fact that this old place is looking nice again."

Kyle grilled hamburgers at dusk while the kids played a game of badminton in his front yard. He'd been feeling lonely for the past two years and thought that Roseanna might be the answer to his prayers when she'd come back to Sulphur last spring. He'd waited a few weeks for her to get her bearings before he moved in and asked her out. He'd thought that surely after the disaster with Trey she wouldn't be nearly as sassy as she'd been back five years ago when they dated.

The same week he'd made up his mind to swoop down and sweep her off her feet, she disappeared for a week. Talk had it that she'd gone off on a freelance tracking job. It wasn't until she came back and Trey had already moved into the lodge that he discovered just who Rosy had been rescuing and why.

He'd gone to the wedding reception and met Greta. Just looking at that woman set his heart to beating too fast and raised his anger up to a dangerous level all at the same time. She was pretty to look at but there wasn't a man on the face of the great green earth who could tame that razor sharp tongue of hers. He was one of the best and he wasn't big enough to get the job done.

An approaching vehicle kicked up a cloud of dust as it rattled down the lane toward his house. For a moment he wondered if LaNita had decided to visit again. She sounded lonely that morning when she called and it would be just like her to hop a plane and rent a car at the airport. He shaded his eyes with the back of his hand and watched. The kids stopped their game and did the same. Greta never looked up.

"It's my parents," Kyle groaned.

Greta laid down the book.

The kids went back to their game.

"Hey, I heard hamburgers were cooking over here. I brought a watermelon basket. Last melon we got of the season. Might as well share it with the lot of you," his mother yelled as she crossed the yard.

His father brought up the rear and carried a huge watermelon that had been carved into a basket, hollowed out, and refilled with fresh fruit.

He sucked in the moan. He most certainly didn't want to introduce Greta to his mother and father. They'd already asked more questions than a sane man could answer in a lifetime. His sister called every day and always, always asked about the convict he was associated with.

"Greta, please let me introduce my parents. This is my mother, Kay Parsons, and my father, Billy Parsons. Mom and Dad, this is Greta Fields, Roseanna's sister-in-law who's been helping me with the youth group," he explained.

"Right glad to know you. I'll just go on inside and put this in the refrigerator," Billy said.

Kay pulled up a lawn chair right beside Greta. "Hot, ain't it? But at least there's a breeze going. We was bound to get a few days of hot yet. Just too early for fall to really be here. So how do you like our area?"

Greta smiled even though she was sick of answering the same question. Did everyone expect her to say that she loved Murray County and planned to sit down and grow roots? She grinned because she could actually feel Kyle's discomfort and that just flat tickled her pink.

"It's a nice place," Greta said.

"Think you'll be staying?"

"Mommmm." Kyle raised an eyebrow.

"Oh, go back to cooking and leave us alone. We're just gettin' to know each other. You don't pay any attention to us. Don't burn those burgers. Kids might not taste scorch but I can," she said.

"I'm going to go do your chores. Be back in half an hour," Billy said from the front door.

"You don't have to do that," Kyle said.

"Don't have to do anything but die and pay taxes. Hold supper for me, son." Billy grinned.

Smart man, his father was. Chores weren't half as bad as sitting and listening to his mother and his . . . what? What was Greta to him? A cohort in youth group? A coworker? Whatever she was, she was certainly not *his* anything.

Too bad since you've already fallen for the woman and just don't know how to accept it, said that niggling voice in the back of his head loud and clear.

"I did not," Kyle mumbled.

"Did not what?" Kay was aware that her son was

very uncomfortable and wondered if he and Greta were arguing. She'd only seen him flustered a few times in his life and, of those times, every one had to do with a woman. He'd been angry enough to tackle a rangy longhorn steer bare-handed when he and Roseanna had argued that night five years before. Evidently, this little dark-haired beauty had gotten under his skin. Kay wasn't sure she liked the idea. Greta Fields came from money and had known a life far and above what Kyle could provide.

"Nothing," Kyle said.

Kay turned back to Greta. "Now, where were we? Oh, talking about you. Tell me about yourself. I understand you had a little wreck and Amos is making you work off the fine doing community service."

"That's right," Greta said. "So, how long have you lived here?"

"I was born here and never lived anywhere else. My grandparents, great-grandparents, and farther back than that lived here. Can't imagine living in any other place. Roots were already set even before I was born."

Greta wasn't a greenhorn in the ways of polite conversation. If she didn't want to answer a wheelbarrow full of questions then she should take the initiative and ask the questions. "How long have you and Mr. Parsons been married?"

"Forty years the day before Christmas. Don't ever do that. Choose a day far away from any holiday as you can. It was romantic at the time, but we never get to have a special anniversary on Christmas Eve. There's cooking to do and presents to wrap up. How do you like living over at Etta's place? Have you met Roxie?" Kay quickly turned the tables.

Greta admired the lady. "The lodge is a nice place to live. We've got a party of ten staying there now until Monday. One of the couples have been married seventy years today."

"God love her heart. She deserves a medal for sure." Kay laughed.

Greta joined her. "She's created a miracle if you ask me."

"Her! What about that poor fool who's put up with her all those years?" Kyle asked.

"Oh, and it's only a fool who can live with a woman that long. Maybe he's been the old codger and she's been a saint," Greta said.

Kay's eyes twinkled.

Kyle threw up his hands in mock defense.

"Back to your questions," Greta said. "Yes, I've met Roxie. Spent Labor Day over at her bed-and-breakfast. At first I thought the house was the ugliest, most garish place I'd ever seen, but it kind of grows on a person, like Roxie does. She and Etta speak their minds and sometimes I don't like what they have to say, but I never have to worry about them talking behind my back."

"That's the truth. Those three old queens had a reputation like that. Molly was my mother's distant relative. Eighth cousins twice removed or some such thing. Never did understand the connection but they were kin some-how. Molly was the other original bed-and-breakfast queen. Died a few months ago with cancer. Anyway, Momma says I'm just like her."

Greta raised an eyebrow.

"Kind of mouthy and prone to speak my mind," Kay explained.

"Amen to that," Kyle said.

Both women shot him a mean look.

"I'll be glad when Dad comes back to give me some help," Kyle said.

"Looks to me like you're doing a fine job of grilling those burgers," Greta said, even though she knew ex-actly what he was thinking.

Kay laughed again.

Greta liked the woman. She'd envisioned Kyle's mother as a little wizened woman who never said a word unless her husband gave her permission. Kay was medium height, had salt-and-pepper hair she wore cut in a fashionable style, wore designer jeans on her slim figure, and a white T-shirt covered with a denim vest decorated with silver studs and black leather laces through silver conchos. Freshly painted red toenails peeked out from leather kitten-heeled sandals and her fingernails were the same color.

By the time they called the youth group to come to supper, Kay and Greta were working together getting the table laid out with condiments, lettuce, freshly sliced tomatoes, Vidalia onions, dill pickles, and potato salad.

Kids sprawled on the living room floor and watched reruns of "Law & Order" while they devoured enough hamburgers to feed a hungry football team after a hard evening of practice. Kay and Greta claimed a spot at the small kitchen table. Billy and Kyle took their plates to the front deck.

"So what do you think of my boy out there?" Kay asked.

"He's a fine man. Some lady will be lucky to get him someday," Greta said.

"Fair enough," Kay said.

"What do you mean?"

"I mean that's enough about Kyle and you. I've danced around the questions all evening and you just put me in my place so I'll leave it alone. No harm done asking. He is a good man, Greta. I hope the lucky lady who winds up with him keeps him on his toes and makes his life interesting. He'd die of boredom if she didn't. Now, could I please ask a favor?"

Greta held her breath.

"Would you please teach these girls how to apply makeup? And give them a few lessons on flirting? They're sadly amiss in both areas."

Greta nodded and swallowed hard.

Kyle parked the truck in front of the lodge. By now he could drive to the lodge in his sleep. His truck could practically make the trip on autopilot without any steering at all.

"I liked your mother and father," Greta said.

"Thank you. Momma is nosy and Dad is quiet." He got out and walked around the back of the truck.

"Your mother loves you," she said when he opened her door. "She wants you to have a wife. She talks around the issue without jumping right in the middle of it."

"I want a wife but I'm a picky man," he said.

They walked to the front door. His hands brushed against hers once, but he quickly took a step to the side so it wouldn't happen again. He wouldn't encourage anything between them ever again. They had very different goals for life and he wasn't tempting fate. A life of misery was what he'd have with Greta, and what he wanted was one of passion and friendship all rolled together.

She turned at the front door. "Anything planned for tomorrow?"

"Not a thing until the Oklahoma City trip."

"Then I'll probably see you in church and then help Jodie in the afternoon. Thank you for a nice day, Kyle. I did enjoy being with the kids and meeting your parents," she said.

Well, would wonders never cease? The woman just thanked him and it sounded genuine, not a bit sarcastic.

"You are welcome." His voice came out hoarse, like his throat was parched and he'd been running a mile.

One moment a foot of open air separated them. The next his arms were around her and his lips were on hers.

The world stood still and the beating of his heart echoed in his ears.

The world spun around in circles and he had to hold her tight to keep from falling from dizziness.

Greta had been kissed before. Lots of times. The first time when she was thirteen and watching her parents' New Year's Eve party from the top of the stairs. The boy was the same age and the kiss dry and unexciting. The exact opposite of the way she felt wrapped in Kyle's arms with his lips on hers. She'd thought the one at the police station was a fluke because she'd been out of the dating game so long, but it hadn't been. This time was proof. She tasted smoked hamburgers, pickles, and the faintest flavor of watermelon.

She wanted the kiss to end so she could break bail and run to a remote island where she'd never see him again, it so unnerved her. In the same moment, she wanted it to go on forever, never end, so she could live forever in his arms.

Finally, he broke away and she slipped from his embrace.

"Good night, Kyle," she said formally.

"Good night," he said just as stiffly.

Neither willing to admit what had just passed between them.

Chapter Eleven

Greta was giddy with excitement, as if she had never been out for an overnight trip before in her life. She, who had traveled to Europe before she started kindergarten, was all excited about a trip to Oklahoma City with a bunch of teenagers. It didn't make a lick of sense but there it was. She suddenly knew what a prisoner must feel like the day he stepped out of the prison walls into freedom. For the first time in three months, she was leaving Murray County. She'd packed her suitcase a dozen times the night before. Before her days of community service, she would have taken fifteen minutes to get ready for a trip like this. She'd taken even less than that the night she drove to Sulphur to attend her brother's wedding.

Kyle glanced over his shoulder from the driver's seat. "Are you aware of why you are here?"

"To help chaperone, of course," she said. They'd settled into a routine that wasn't comfortable by any means, yet wasn't uncomfortable either: a state of limbo in which both of them put the feelings evoked by a couple of kisses into a mental box, shoved it back into the attic of their minds, and tried desperately to pretend it never happened. She didn't want to admit her world had been shaken so hard it had almost shattered. She'd slept poorly that night and kept stealing glances at him through church the next day. Every time the phone rang Sunday afternoon, she jumped. When Etta called out her name and said someone wanted to speak to her, she had a speech all ready about how it was just a kiss of the moment, like the one in the station house, and not to be taken seriously. It had been her mother on the other end. She could have wept.

"Yes, that's why you are here. Let me rephrase the question. Do you have any idea how you got here?" he asked.

She cocked her head to one side and frowned. He'd picked her up for work every day the whole month and it was pure business. Not one word other than brief discussions about the weather. This morning hadn't been a lot different, except there were ten kids in the van. Had he suddenly gone stupid?

"What are you talking about? You arrived not twenty minutes ago to the lodge. That's how I got in the van."

He shook his head. "Kelsey bribed the judge."

Surely Greta heard him wrong. She shot a quick glance over her shoulder. Boys on one side talking about fishing lures and deer hunting. Girls in the back two seats, giggling about lipstick and shoes. Then she leaned over to the left as far as the seat belt allowed. "She did what? She bribed the judge? Judge Amos?"

Kyle nodded. "She's his babysitter and he needs her to keep his kids all day in a week or two so he and his wife can attend a wedding in Tulsa. She said she would but he had to let you go on this trip. He accused her of bribery and she said it was just a fact. If you didn't get to go she would be sick that weekend and he could find himself another babysitter. So that's why you are here."

Her ego deflated. "When he called me to say he was lifting the ban for just these two days he said it was because Wilma had given him glowing reports of how hard I'd been working. I thought I'd scored some points with him."

"Now you know. Do you think he'd admit he'd been conned by a thirteen-year-old?"

She leaned back and stared out the side window without seeing a thing. No one had ever done such a thing for her before. Monica, her very best friend in Tulsa, wouldn't even go to her apartment and send a credit card and some underpants. She was too afraid of her father cutting off her own monetary sources, and here a child had stood up to a judge just so Greta could go on a youth group trip with them. She had trouble swallowing the lump in her throat and keeping the tears at bay.

They reached the Omniplex at ten o'clock and were some of the first people inside. All ten teenagers had already taken a poll and voted to spend their time in the space and aviation section. Kelsey and Jim both had decided in the last year that they were going to be astronauts when they grew up. Andy was going to fly crop dusters for his grandfather's business and the rest of the crew didn't care what part of the Omni they visited.

Kyle and Greta hung back and gave them free rein. First they went to the historical section, which interested Andy since one of the planes resembled a crop duster. They looked at the Lockheed F-104 Starfighter, the Ryan PT-22, and a Fokker triplane painted the same shade of red as Roxie's house. Those folks who designed and built the original planes sure wanted them to be seen in the sky. No light gray for these planes; bright turquoise, brilliant blues, and golds made them very visible.

"Maybe I'll be a crop duster too," Cathy said. "I want a hot pink airplane with glitter on the wings."

"Girls can't be crop dusters," Andy argued.

Cathy bowed up to him. "I can do anything you can."

Kyle spoke for the first time since he'd told Greta about Kelsey and the judge. "Do you believe that?"

"Believe what?"

"That you could be a crop duster?"

"If I wanted to fly that red plane right there out of

this building, I'd dang sure do it. Women can do anything men can. Cathy is right."

Kyle chuckled.

She stared right into his pecan-colored eyes. "You don't believe me?"

"Yes, ma'am, I surely do believe you. That's why men run from you," he said.

"Men don't run from me. They run to me."

"Only to find out you're bold, sassy, and hard to live with."

"You are not going to ruin my day so forget it. I'm happy today and I'm going to enjoy it." She headed in the direction of the girls and ignored him the rest of the morning.

Greta happy? Now that was an oxymoron. Happy in the company of what she referred to as a small-town cop when she was in a generous mood and who knew what other adjectives she applied when she was ticked off at him. Kyle shook his head but the idea didn't dislodge. Greta happy? Hmmm.

They had lunch at the Spaghetti Warehouse in Bricktown. They were seated in the real railroad dining car located in the middle of the restaurant. Four tables for four lined one side of the narrow dining car. On the other side there were also four tables but only for two people with a narrow center aisle between them. The kids split up into groups and took up three tables. Greta and Kyle chose a table for two.

"Do we have a budget?" Cathy asked when the

waitress brought menus and sourdough bread with special herbed butter.

"Not today," Kyle said. "The senior citizen Sunday school group handed me a check before we left and said for you to have a meal on them."

"What can I get you to drink?" the waitress asked.

"I guess that doesn't mean we can have a glass of wine, does it?" Andy teased.

Kyle shook his head.

"Then Coke is fine." Andy laughed.

"Do you need more time to study the menu?"

"No, ma'am," Andy said. "I'm hungry. I want this right here." He pointed to the menu.

It didn't take the others long to follow suit or to dive right into the bread and butter.

"And for you two?" the waitress asked Kyle.

"I'll have the manicotti. Honey mustard dressing on my salad. Sweet tea with lots of ice," Greta said.

Kyle handed her the menu. "Make it the same."

"So you like Italian?"

"Love it. Manicotti. Spaghetti. Lasagna. Rigatoni. All of it," he said.

She nodded and read the rectangular advertisements around the rounded top of the box car. One read "Blessed are the youth for they shall inherit the national debt."

"Do you think Herbert Hoover really said that?" she pointed.

"He's got the credit, evidently," Kyle answered.

She lowered her voice. "Speaking of the youth, what is this trip teaching them?"

He sipped the tea the waitress brought with more bread. "Airplanes. Getting along in public places. Sharing time. Not whining when they have to do something for someone else. Lots of things."

Using the oversized steak knife, she cut the loaf of sourdough bread into inch-thick slabs. She slathered one with butter and shut her eyes when she ate it. "This is so good. I wonder if Etta ever makes sourdough bread."

Kyle buttered a chunk for himself. "If she can't I bet Roxie has a recipe. Between the three of them, they could make anything."

Lunch arrived and the noise in the kids' corner died down.

Greta looked at the platter, half white and half red. "I forgot to tell the lady I wanted all white on my manicotti."

"I don't like white. I like red. Want to share?" Kyle asked.

"Sure. We can trade," she said.

For a moment it felt like they were an old familiar couple out on a date. High color filled her cheeks. Dating Kyle wasn't even an option; not that he'd want to date her anyway. So they'd gotten caught up in the moment and shared a couple of kisses. It didn't mean there was enough common ground to withstand even one date.

"Dessert anyone?" The waitress refilled glasses.

"Kyle?" Kelsey asked.

He nodded.

"Then I want one of these tiramisu things. But I can't eat all of it. Anyone want to share?"

"I'll share with you," Jim said.

"I want a cheesecake and I want all of it," Andy said.

When she had the orders for the kids, she turned again to Kyle and Greta.

"Tiramisu, but I can't eat all of it, either," Greta said.

"We'll share one. Bring us two forks," Kyle ordered.

Eating with Kyle, dipping her fork into the ladyfingers and fillings, was far more intimate than she wanted to admit. She should have ordered her own dessert and eaten every bite of it even if it made her sick. Her fingertips brushed his more than once and the electricity that lit up the place seemed almost visible.

By the time they checked into the Clarion Motel, confusion filled her heart. She should have stayed at home. Being alone with Kyle, even in the midst of a crowd, wasn't such a good idea, especially when she hadn't been out on a date since the first of summer. First it was Trey in trouble with the kidnapping incident, then it was the company's downsizing and Greta trying to find a job without any luck. After that Trey announced he and Rosy were getting married again and she had to go the wedding. The rest was in the history books: page one about a bull that died north of Sulphur. If there really was a book like that she wondered what page two would have.

The girls had two rooms with a connecting door in the motel. They threw their suitcases on the queen-sized beds and went to digging for their bathing suits. Cathy claimed first rights to a bathroom and came out in a hot pink two piece that showed her cute little figure off. The boys would all be posturing for her attention for sure. Kelsey, next in line, wore a black mallot dipped low in the back. She tugged a T-shirt with Tweety Bird on the front over her suit and grabbed a towel from the rack beside the bathroom door. Sueann wore a baby pink tankini covered with big yellow daisies. Molly's suit was faded from a dark blue to a nondescript color.

"Momma said I couldn't buy a new one this late in the year because next year I'll need a bigger size," she explained with a blush.

Greta felt terrible for staring.

Amber shook her finger at Molly. "Hey, stop apologizing. If we had a pool in our backyard ours would be faded too. We only get to go swimming when we can talk our folks into taking us to the park. I can't wait until I can drive."

"Then you can all four come and swim in my pool anytime you want," Molly said.

Greta picked up a book and followed them to the pool. The boys were already there and were playing around with a ball. They had the area to themselves so Greta had her choice of lawn chairs. She chose one as far away from the splashing water as possible and stretched her legs out.

Kyle showed up in a bathing suit and a loose-fitting T-shirt with a towel draped over his shoulder. "So you're not swimming?"

"Not today. I'm going to read and maybe nap."

"Can't swim?"

"Can. Don't want to."

He sat down in a chair beside her. "Four more weeks and your sentence is up."

"Can't get here fast enough."

"Question. If I'd been some kind of oil executive and lived in, say, Tulsa, or maybe even Dallas, and we'd met in different circumstances, and I asked you out to dinner, would you have gone?"

She was baffled. Her mouth went dry and her ears were ringing. "But we didn't meet in different circumstances so I don't know what I would have done. Would you have asked me?"

"I don't know."

He didn't say that when he had looked across the corral at the wedding reception and had seen her that his heart had actually hurt for a few minutes. That he'd covered up the attraction with jokes or that he had made it a point to be only businesslike for the past month but was still attracted to her. He sure didn't say that in spite of her position both as a parolee and a very rich lady, he couldn't get her out of his mind and dreamed about her nearly every night.

She didn't tell him how just the touch of his fingertips over tiramisu affected her. The silence hung between them like a heavy shroud. There were things that needed saying, but neither of them could utter a word.

"So tell me about Kelsey. What makes her brave enough to stand up to the judge like that?" She tried to put the conversation on more familiar, less painful ground and end the uncomfortable silence that was suffocating her.

"Kelsey comes from a broken family. Her father disappeared when she was just a baby and her mother keeps the family together by working two jobs. She's a teller at one of the banks by day and works as a waitress in the evenings. Kelsey is the youngest of three. The other two have already graduated. Her sister is married and her brother goes to college. They help out when they can and she babysits for the judge's little girls for extra money."

"And Molly?"

"Molly comes from a wealthy family. She's an only child but not spoiled. Her mother and father earned their money. They didn't inherit it. They're older. Cathy was born when her mother was well past forty and they'd given up on ever having a child. Surprises me she's not rotten to the core, but they've done a good job with her."

"Sueann?" Anything to keep him talking. She'd never noticed how soothing the deep timbre of his voice was.

"Sueann has a mother and father who are ranchers. She's the oldest of four children. All of the others are boys and wilder than a Texas tornado. She's a rodeo girl. Barrel races and thinks Jodie Cahill is only a notch below God."

"Cathy?"

"Lives with her grandmother. Her mother wasn't married when she was born. Was killed in a car wreck when Cathy was two or three years old. Her grandmother has raised her ever since. My turn now, what about us?"

Greta jerked her head around to stare at him. Had he really just said what she thought she heard?

"What did you ask?" She frowned, her dark eyebrows knitting into a solid line above her troubled brown eyes.

"I asked, what about us? We've been avoiding the physical attraction for a solid month. What do you think about us?"

"There is no us, Kyle. It was a couple of kisses. Adults do that sometimes. It doesn't mean you have to make an honest woman out of me and drop down on one knee."

"I know that, but there's something there, Greta. Something bigger than a couple of kisses."

She inhaled deeply. "Maybe, but if there was, what could we do about it? Not what would we do, but what could we do? I'm not ever going to live in Sulphur, Oklahoma. I'd wither up and die and resent the devil out of everyone around me. You're a small-town policeman and rancher in the making. You'd be as out of place in my world as Roseanna was in Trey's. So there's a bit of attraction. We'll learn to ignore it."

"I suppose you are right. Glad we cleared that up," he said.

"Me too."

"Momma says you're helping her at the Halloween carnival tomorrow night. Selling chili to make money for her Sunday school class," Kyle said.

"Yes, I am. She asked me last Sunday after church and I told her I'd be glad to help. Never been to a Halloween festival but I'm willing to give it a try. Over in Davis, right?"

"That's right." Kyle smiled. She'd just admitted she had feelings for him without saying the actual words. That was something to build on and he had a whole month before Thanksgiving.

Five girls lined the stools in front of the Clinique counter at Dillard's. The salesclerks draped them in capes and began a makeover on each girl, teaching them the basic techniques of applying makeup as they went. By the time they finished the girls were oohing and aahing over everything.

"And would you girls like to purchase any of the items we've used?" a perky little saleslady asked.

"I'd like to know about the free kit you are offering," Greta said.

"It's a fifty-five-dollar, basic makeup kit in a cute little Clinique tote bag. It's called "All About Eyes Rich" and has eye shadow, mascara, lipstick, an eyelash curler, and rinse-off eye makeup solvent. It's a free gift with a minimum purchase of twenty-one-fifty," the lady said.

Greta pointed toward the end of the counter. "We'll take five of those compacts. Do the girls need to pay separately or can I cover it in one bill? And would you please put them in separate bags?"

"I can ring it up separately and you can pay for it all at once and we'll be glad to bag it separately."

"Thank you, Greta," the girls chorused in surprised voices.

"You are very welcome. Remember what she taught you. Makeup is to enhance your beauty and you are all gorgeous already." She peeled six twenty-dollar bills and a five from her wallet, wishing the whole time she could have purchased more than a compact for each girl. But just that much cost a chunk of what she'd worked so hard to earn the past month. The saleslady handed Greta back a few coins.

Kelsey led the way out of the store. "Now that we are beautiful, let's go to try on clothes."

They met Kyle and the guys meandering up the mall with hang dog faces. One hour down and two to go.

"Are y'all really going to make us stay in here the whole time?" Jim asked.

Greta pointed a finger at him. "No whining."

"We can be nice. Greta was nice to us so we'll be nice to you. Right girls?" Sueann asked.

"Depends on your definition of nice," Kelsey said.

"We want to go to a couple of stores but we'd also

like to go to the Ross store in the strip mall before we leave, so if you all can entertain yourselves for one hour we'll go over there and you can play in the bookstore or the pet store. Deal?"

"Pet store is better than this place. One hour. We'll be waiting right here." He pointed toward a seating area in front of Dillard's.

"How about you?" Kyle asked Greta.

"I imagine they can shop without me." She said, then turned to the girls. "Stay in a group, girls. No wandering off alone. And, Kelsey, you're the one responsible to get everyone back here in one hour," Greta said.

"So you're staying with us?" Jim asked.

"No, we're going down the mall and sitting down at the first place that sells good coffee," Kyle told them.

"Next time I'm not betting with those girls," Andy declared.

Kyle bought two cups of coffee and they sat on a comfortable sofa in a different seating area than the boys. "Tell me what you were like as a child," he said.

"Why?"

"To fill up an hour and keep me entertained," he said.

"According to my mother, I was a difficult child. Always competing with Trey. Never happy unless I could do better than he'd done when it came to grades, tennis, golf—anything at all. According to my father, I've been a cross to bear. Always in trouble for driving too fast and not doing exactly what he wanted. According to Trey, I'm a brat. That's it in a nutshell."

"Well, what are we going to do with the next fifty minutes?" He smiled.

Kyle was so handsome when he smiled and his brown eyes lit up. She'd noticed it the first time she bumped into him at the reception. She sipped her coffee and watched an elderly couple with a little girl about four years old. The girl skipped along in front of the couple but kept looking back to make sure they hadn't disappeared. When they were close enough she called them Nanny and Poppa.

Greta remembered her grandmother taking her shopping. Usually in a very exclusive little shop in Dallas where the clerks fawned over her. She could never remember skipping in a mall with both grandparents watching out after her.

"One minute gone. Forty-nine more. Bored yet?" Kyle asked.

"Do you want children?" She blushed as soon as the words were out of her mouth. Good grief, had she really said that out loud? Lately she couldn't curb her tongue at all. If she thought something, it was instantly out in the open.

"Of course, I want children. Is this a proposal?"

"It is not. I was just watching that little girl and felt a yearning to have a daughter. I love being with the girls this weekend. At first I thought I was caught up in the moment of it all, but that's not what it is at all. I'm having a good time," she said.

A wide grin split his face again.

She wished he'd stop that.

"Kyle, you are a youth director. Don't look at me like that!" she exclaimed.

"And you're the lady who killed my bull. If I can get past that, maybe you can get past my volunteer job."

"And what about LaNita?"

"What's she got to do with anything?"

"She thinks she's your wife. How do you divorce a person who's a wife but not a wife?" she asked.

A frown replaced the smile. "I guess you just tell her the friendship is a lot different now."

"Well, you'd better tell her before you start flirting with me."

"Are you jealous?" Kyle asked.

"No, I'd have to care to be jealous. I'm simply getting you ready for some unlucky lady in the future," she lied.

Chapter Twelve

The weatherman said the cold snap would pull the temperature down to fifty-five degrees that night, but he missed the mark. By the time the Halloween parade started the thermometer on the side of the bank declared it was fifty degrees. A slight north wind dropped the chill factor a few degrees lower than that.

Greta wore jeans and a T-shirt and had pulled a gray hooded sweatshirt over her head. Before the parade began, she and Kay had found their designated spot on the north side of the roped-off street in front of The Davis Florist shop. They organized an eight-foot folding table with a Crock-Pot of chili on each end, Styrofoam bowls and plastic spoons in between, along with bottles of mustard and jars of jalapeño peppers for those who were definitely not fainthearted.

186

Rules said that they wouldn't sell until half an hour after the parade. "But by getting set up early we can watch the kids and be ready for the first onslaught. Weather this cold, everyone is going to want chili to warm them up. I hear the fire siren. Come on. I love to watch the kids, especially when the theme is Disney characters," Kay said.

"Who would you be if you were a little girl in this parade?" Kyle asked so close to her ear the warmth of his breath was like hot coals on her neck.

She hadn't known he'd planned to come to the festival and sure hadn't felt his presence, but she shivered when he spoke. "The Little Mermaid," she said.

"Why? Because you are a fish out of the water of your big city?" he asked.

"Because I can't live here," she answered. "What do those numbers mean on their backs?"

"Long or short answer?" he asked.

"It doesn't matter."

"Each class in the school elects a boy and girl to walk in the parade. Their parents are responsible for the costumes. Interspersed throughout the crowd are judges who decide which ones are the best and they judge by the number on the child's back. There will be a prince and princess from the lower grades and a king and queen from the upper ones in the elementary school. The rest of the participants have been entered for the ugliest, the cutest, etc. Those folks over there with the cameras are taking pictures for the newspaper next week. This is a big thing in both Sulphur, who had their carnival last night, and here in Davis."

"Why didn't the church sell chili last night?"

"We did," Kay said. "Roxy and Dee manned the table in Sulphur. Sold out in less than an hour but couldn't go home. They had Bodine and several of her friends with them as well as Jack, who loves Halloween carnivals."

"What about Jaxson?"

"Right there." Kyle pointed.

Jack wore black sweatpants and a hooded shirt, and pulled Jaxson in a red Ryder wagon with wooden sideboards. The baby's costume was a bright orange pumpkin complete with a green stem on his little hat, and he looked as if he'd really grown there in a bed of loose hay.

Jaxson grinned at his adoring public, showing off four baby teeth, two upper and two lower, and commenced tossing hay over the side of the wagon. A deep yearning set up home in her heart. She wanted one of those. A baby to ride in a Halloween parade in a small town.

No, I do not. I might want a baby but not in a small town. I'm getting too quick to let myself be caught up in the excitement of the moment. A handsome man standing beside me. Adorable children everywhere I look. What woman wouldn't have an attack of Iwannababyitis?

"Did you go to the one in Sulphur last night after we got home from Oklahoma City?" Greta asked Kyle.

"No, I did chores at the house and went to bed early. Knew there would be one over here tonight and that Momma might need some help," he said.

"You think I can't dip chili or take money?" She picked a fight. Anything to put them on familiar ground and away from the place where she was thinking he was handsome and babies were desirable.

"You can't talk on a phone and drive. What's the difference?" He shot right back. What on earth made her go from all nice to mean in five seconds?

"Stop fighting. Here come the decorated bicycles and that's the last thing, so let's man the tables and get ready for the first customers," Kay said.

Ten minutes later people were standing in line. Kay and Greta both filled bowls as fast as they could. Kyle took money and made change. When the cookers were near empty, Kay motioned at Kyle and he brought two more full ones to the table and returned the empties to Kay's truck. Only once in the next hour did they have a break in buyers. That was when the judges announced the title winners of the parade. Jaxson won cutest costume in his category. Cinderella and Prince Charming were crowned prince and princess. Beauty and the Beast were the new Halloween king and queen.

Jack bought the last bowl of chili, warmed it up with two spoonfuls of jalapeños, and sat down on the curb in front of the flower shop to eat it. Bodine came by at one time and Greta noticed she shook her head violently when he offered her a bite.

Kyle grabbed her hand. "Walk with me and we'll see if there's any food left anywhere."

"You mean we're not going home now?"

"Of course not. We haven't even done the haunted house. And you've got to have an Indian taco if they're still cooking them. It's the primary reason I come to this carnival."

"What is an Indian taco?"

"Ahhh, you are in for a treat." He led her across the street and to the corner where a team of ladies cooked on a couple of electric grills.

"Thought you were going to miss out, Kyle. Two?" the older lady asked.

"I was afraid I would when I found Momma had brought four cookers of chili. Fix up three. Two for me and one for the lady."

"Hi, honey. Glad to see Kyle is finally dating again. He's too good a man to waste." She handed him two plates covered with fried bread.

He had to let go of Greta's hand to take them.

Greta reached out and took her plate from the woman's hand and didn't even bother to explain that she was not Kyle's date. Her stomach growled. Hunger before pseudo romance. Besides, he heard the comment and hadn't contradicted it.

"Follow me," Kyle said. He covered the bread with scrumptious smelling taco meat from a big cooker and proceeded down the table, layering lettuce, tomatoes, cheese, sour cream, refried beans, and fresh salsa on top of the bread.

Greta followed suit and followed him to an empty piece of the curb where they balanced paper plates on their laps and ate with plastic forks. "Mmmm." She made appreciative noises with every bite. "This is better than the manicotti at Spaghetti Warehouse."

When she finished, she scooted closer to Kyle and shared his second one without asking. While they were engaged in a battle of the forks to see who got the last bite, Jodie sat down beside her, reached across, and nabbed it with her fingers.

"I settled that argument," Jodie said when she'd swallowed. "I love those things. I've already had two tonight and my mouth is watering for another one but my stomach is too full to eat it."

Kyle pointed across the street at a table in front of the Specialty Bakery. "I'm going for fresh-squeezed lemonade right over there. Either of you want one?"

Both women nodded.

"So you and Kyle are an item, huh?"

"We are not!" Greta exclaimed loudly.

"Looks like it to me," Jodie said.

"We were helping Kay and then he asked me if I wanted a taco . . ." Greta stammered.

"He held your hand across the street. He bought your supper. He's off getting lemonade. You are sitting with him. The old ladies are already making bets when you'll have him in a tux and waiting at the front of the church," Jodie said.

"This is not the dark ages." Greta was still stuttering.

Kyle darted between people and brought two tall paper cups of lemonade to the ladies.

"Thank you so much. I'm going to find Trey and Rosy. Trey won a big old German chocolate cake on the cake walk and Rosy can't get him away from the cake walk now. He's got his eye on a three-tiered black forest and he'll be walking around that circle until it's gone." Jodie headed down the street with a wave.

"Drink up. They're starting another tour through the haunted house in ten minutes. I stopped and bought tickets while I was on that side of the street," Kyle said.

She'd been in haunted houses before so she stoically resolved not to scream no matter how many plastic spiders fell from the ceiling right in front of her nose. He'd see that no backwoodsy country haunted house could terrify her. She'd helped her friends make them in their two-, three-, four- or five-car garages for Halloween parties when she was a teenager.

Her determination lasted thirty seconds. The first time a real human-type person threw open the lid of a black coffin and raised up, she squealed. When an evil-looking man revved up a chain saw and it looked exactly like he cut a woman in half, blood spraying everywhere, she buried her face in Kyle's chest and shuddered. Before they reached the back door, he was holding her close to his side with an arm around her waist.

Out in the cool night air on a side street, she gasped, the vision of murder and mayhem still in her mind. "How did they do that? I thought that man really cut that woman up with the chain saw. That was the scariest thing I've ever done."

"Hey, y'all want to go again?" Bodine and her friends exited right behind Greta and Kyle.

"No!" Greta said.

"You mean they don't have haunted houses in Tulsa?"

Greta kept a tight grip on Kyle's hand. "Not like that."

"We're going to get some lemonade and do it again." The girls took off in a trot. A couple of years ago they would have been running. In a couple more they'd be too grown up to walk fast.

"To answer your questions, the chain saw wasn't even really turned on. Those flashing lights made you think it was, but it was an illusion. The noise was from a CD player in the room. The woman's head was the only thing that was real in that scenario. She was actually sitting on her knees under the table with her head poking up through a hole, and the rest of her body was fake. The blood was ketchup and the rest of it came from the meatpacking plant. Leftovers from hog butchering."

"How gruesome. I'm surprised people let their kids go in there," she said.

"Everyone knows it's just fun," Kyle assured her. "Want to go again now that you know what it is?"

"Not on your life!"

"Want another taco?"

"After that chain saw incident, I may not eat for a week."

"How about trying your luck on the cake walk?"

"Okay." She nodded. That sounded safe enough. Surely there were no chain saws or screaming heads involved in something that simple.

Kyle led her up the street a block and bought a dozen tickets. "When the music starts you walk around the circle. When it stops, you stop on a number. They pull a piece of paper from a hat and if you are on the number they draw, you get the next cake in the row," he explained.

She looked at the dozen cakes still lined up on the table. The next one was a lovely Italian crème with cream cheese icing. She wouldn't mind taking that home for a midnight snack. She stood on number twenty-five, her lucky number according to the palm reader she'd seen in Las Vegas last winter. Kyle parked his feet on number twelve, which was right behind her. She pulled her hand free of his. No way was he going to push her on or hold her back. This was serious business. That cake was already hers. She'd made the decision when she saw Trey across the circle giving her the old sibling rivalry look.

The music began. Trey won the Italian crème but in the very next walk she won the black forest cake. After ten minutes of bantering, they traded.

Kyle carried her cake a block south to where he'd left his truck in the Baptist church parking lot. He carefully set it on the floor in the backseat of the double-cab black truck and drove slowly on the back streets to get out of town.

"Was this a date?" she asked bluntly when he was on the highway headed east toward Sulphur.

"Do you want it to be a date?"

"I asked first," she said.

"Did I ask you for a date?"

Greta turned around in the seat and checked her cake. It was in a disposable aluminum pan. Trey's was on a cardboard circle. She hoped he had to hold it in his lap the whole way and Rosy hit every pothole in the road. "No, but Jodie said it looked like one to her."

"Then it was a date. We wouldn't want Jodie to be wrong, would we? Not since she's your very best friend."

"I barely tolerate Jodie. She's my brother's sister-in-law and I've never liked her."

"But she grows on you, doesn't she?" Kyle said.

"Are you taking up for her? Sounds like maybe you wish this was a date with her?" Greta snapped around, ignoring the cake and wishing for once she could control her wicked temper.

"Okay, enough of what this person thinks or that, or even how we feel. I really, really did not like you in the beginning. You were abrasive, demanding, spoiled, and everything else I don't like in a woman."

"But?" She held her breath and her temper, amazed that she wasn't fighting mad already.

"But I've watched you change, Greta. You speak your

mind but so does my mother. You are a giving woman with the kids in the youth group as well as with Wilma. Your heart is good and I like you. I'd like to date you, that's a fact, but it would be a heartbreaker, because I really believe that you would be unhappy in my world and I know I'd be miserable in yours. I think there's heartstrings between us that could be encouraged to grow and produce a good relationship."

"But . . . ," she said again.

"But in order to have that relationship one of us would have to give up their life. I'm tied to this place. I have land, cattle, a home, and a job I love. You are just as tied to your big-city life. It won't work, but that doesn't mean I don't like you."

"I understand," she said.

Whew! A miracle had just happened right there on the highway between Davis and Sulphur. Kyle Parsons admitted he'd had a change of opinion and didn't hate her anymore. Her heart floated all the way to the clouds, skipping across the moon. Of course, he was right in everything he'd said. The man lived in a trailer house far out in the country. His day began and ended with chores and cows and police work in the middle. His idea of a date was a Halloween carnival.

She'd had a wonderful evening and couldn't remember a time when she'd felt so alive or happy. Dinner at the most expensive restaurant in Tulsa and dancing afterward couldn't have held as much excitement as eating Indian tacos from a paper plate while sitting on the street curb and then going through that gory haunted house. But it would never work on the long haul for a lifetime. She'd be bored to tears in six months.

"Pretty quiet. You usually have a biting remark about everything," he said.

"My father could give you a job in the security part of his business," she mumbled.

"Is that a proposal?"

"It is not!"

He made a right-hand turn into the park and a few miles farther, another right on to Cahill Ranch and Lodge property. He parked the truck in the usual spot and walked her to the porch. Instead of leaving, though, he sat down on the steps. "Greta, what are we going to do about this?"

She sat down beside him but was very careful to keep a foot of night air between them. "We already had this discussion once, didn't we? We'd just be rehashing it if we talked about it any more."

He threw an arm around her shoulders and drew her close. "I suppose so, but if this was a date, then I should at least have a good-night kiss."

She looked up at the same time he bent forward and their lips met in one of those fiery kisses that heated up the chill of the night.

When he released her he brushed a sweet kiss right between her eyes. "So good-night and sweet dreams. I'll save you a seat in church tomorrow morning."

"Kyle," she moaned.

"Hey, they're already saying we're dating. Might as well have the game if we are going to have the name. Besides, like you said yesterday. We're adults. We can enjoy each other's company for a few weeks and say good-bye like big people do. It's not like we are going into this blind, is it?"

"So we are dating for the next four weeks and then we will shake hands and go our separate ways?" she asked.

"Might as well. You got anything better to do?"

"I suppose not."

"Good, then after church would you care to join me for lunch?"

"I'd love to," she said.

"Bring a change of clothes. Jeans, a shirt, and boots. We'll go riding after lunch."

"Okay." She nodded. "Good night, Kyle. And I really did have a good time this evening."

"Don't ever tell me there's not magic out on Halloween night. Greta Fields just spent the evening with me and said she enjoyed it." He chuckled.

"Go home before we fight," she threw over her shoulder as she shut the door behind her.

She slid down the back of the door and put her head in her hands. "What have I done? I'm about to get my heart broken."

Chapter Thirteen

Several eyebrows raised when Greta sat with Kyle in church. Kelsey winked. Molly whispered to Sueann. None of the boys noticed. Roxy gave her a knowing look. Jodie grinned and nodded.

No one understood that this was just a passing fancy.

She wore her new broomstick skirt made of bronze silk with beadwork around the hem. The knit shirt was the same color with the same type of work around the bottom. At least it was something new if she did have to lay out half a week's paycheck to purchase it. She'd found a pair of heels the same night on the half-price table. All of it from the local Wal-Mart store. None of it had designer tags, but she felt pretty that morning.

Kyle shared the hymn book with her and after church told Etta he'd have her home before bedtime. Etta said that she had a key and knew how to get inside the lodge. No guests were scheduled until after Thanksgiving. She and Roxie left together for lunch at The Bread Basket, a restaurant connected to the casino out west of Davis.

Greta buckled her seat belt. "Where are we having lunch?"

"We'll be eating at the finest establishment in the county, milady. Momma put a ham in the oven this morning. Both of my sisters are tied up on Thanksgiving Day so we're having our big thing today. Then on the actual day, Momma and Dad are going to Austin for the whole week. Roxie has invited me to eat with her family so I won't be left out in the cold."

Greta's ears actually popped as if she'd been on top of a mountain. "Your family, all of them are going to be at this dinner?"

"That's right. They were late getting to church. My sister, Mary, will be late to her own funeral, I swear, but at least dinner will be on time because Momma takes care of it. Do you like pumpkin pie?"

"Your family? Kyle, just take me to Etta's and I'll have a peanut butter sandwich. They'll think . . ."

"What? That you are my date? Well, you are, you know. It's not a proposal, Greta. Just a date. Play along with it so they'll get off my back and stop trying to fix me up with every woman in the whole U.S. of A. Mary's husband has a dozen female cousins. Misty's husband has even more. Just be my date and be nice to me so they'll leave me alone."

"And the payment is?"

"All the turkey and dressing and pumpkin pie you can eat," he said.

"Do I have to fawn over you or sneak little kisses on the cheek or any other disgusting things?"

"Disgusting?"

She giggled. "Okay. No kissing. I'll be the perfect date and you'll owe me a big favor. Like stopping at Wal-Mart on the way home one night next week."

"You got it."

"Why didn't you tell me this last night when you asked me?" she asked.

"Because you wouldn't have agreed. You barely did when you thought it was just going to be the two of us in a restaurant. How good are you at acting? They'll spot a fake a mile away," he said.

"Oh, I'm very, very good at acting. You just play along with me and by the day's end you'll be safe from all their cousins," she teased.

He whistled as he parked, opened the truck door for her, took her hand in his and walked up on the porch where the men folks sipped iced tea and waited for the ladies to call them to dinner. "I'd like to introduce you to Greta Fields. Greta, this is my sister Mary's husband, Luke, and their son, Stephen. This is my sister Misty's husband, Derrick. They have a daughter, Lizzy, who is probably in the house. You've already met my dad."

"Hello," she said sweetly.

The men muttered niceties and Stephen blushed his way through a "nice to meet you, ma'am."

Kyle ushered her into the house. "Okay, honey, now let's go meet the ladies."

"Honey?" she whispered with an edge to her tone.

"Remember it's a trip to Wal-Mart on the way home."

"Yes, darlin'," she growled.

"Hey, y'all, I want you to meet Greta. She works with me at the station. Greta, this is my sister, Mary, the one stirring the beans. That's Misty over there setting the table and my niece, Lizzy, slicing bread. All of you, this is Greta Fields."

"Are you with Uncle Kyle today?" Lizzy looked up. Dark hair hung in naturally curly ringlets around her oval face. Her eyes were light brown and she had dimples.

"Yes, I am," Greta told the lie so smooth it sounded like the truth even to her.

She looked at her mother. "See, I told you to leave him alone and he'd find his own girlfriend, and she's prettier than any of Daddy's relatives too."

Kay laughed. "Out of the mouths of babes, but this one is eleven years old so she's scarcely a babe anymore. Come on in here, Greta. You can run the mixer in this bowl of potatoes. When they're smooth add some butter and sour cream."

"So what do you do at the station?" Mary asked.

"I'm on parole. I was driving much too fast and talking on a cell phone. I dropped it and lost control when I tried to pick it up off the floor. Wound up in a ditch with your brother screaming and yelling about his bull."

Lizzy's eyes bugged out. "That was you!"

"Good God!" Misty said.

"He called you a—"

Kay clamped her hand over Lizzy's mouth. "I've got a bar of soap if your mouth gets dirty."

"I didn't say it. Uncle Kyle did," she protested.

"Well, don't life turn round," Mary said. "A word of advice from the oldest sister. Don't be all sugar bear and honey pie with my brother. He's a handful and it'll take a special woman to lasso him, girl. Someone to push him right out to the edge of the cliff and then jerk him back if he starts to jump."

Greta was stunned into silence at Mary's recommendation. Trey had called her a brat in front of other people all the time, but she'd never expected Kyle's sisters to do anything but sing his little praises from the rooftops.

"Yes, ma'am," Greta whispered.

They were seated together around the dining room table for the meal. The turkey setting in a bed of corn-bread dressing was the centerpiece. Candied yams, baked beans, cranberry salad, hot rolls, green beans with bacon, and new potatoes, mashed potatoes, and the list went on. Kyle's father carved the turkey. Plates were passed. Everyone talked at once. Greta loved every moment of it.

"So how did you two decide to like each other after such a meeting?" Lizzy asked loud enough that the room went stone-cold silent and all eyes were on Greta and Kyle.

Kyle leaned over to brush a kiss on Greta's cheek. "You tell them the story, honey."

"Well, it all happened the night we had to go out to this house where an old couple were having a custody fight over a cat named Riggs." She deliberately bit into a hot roll, hoping they'd begin to talk again and forget about her and Kyle.

They didn't.

She swallowed. "The husband and wife each had a butcher knife and were circling a big bush. They kept on worrying about who was going to take care of their cat, Riggs, as we took them back to jail. Anyway, we started laughing about it and found we weren't mad about the wreck anymore. Kyle forgave me for killing his bull and I forgave him for acting like a jerk over it," she said sweetly.

His jaws worked in anger. How dare she say he was a jerk in front of his family. They'd be selling Jack Daniel's inside the Pearly Gates before she got him to take her to Wal-Mart next week.

"That's not romantic," Lizzy said. "Momma and Daddy met at a rodeo and she took one look at him and knew he was the man she was going to marry someday. They were only ten years old but she ran him to the ground by the time they were twenty-one."

"Straight from the mouth of her mother," Derrick said. "Now, tell me, Kay, how's the pecan crop looking this year? Think we could find a few to take back to Austin before we leave tomorrow?"

Lizzy groaned. "I don't want to spend my afternoon picking up pecans. I want to go riding with Uncle Kyle and Greta."

"Sorry, kid. You want divinity candy for the real Thanksgiving, you got to pick up pecans with the rest of us," Kay said.

Greta and Kyle finished their meal without having to answer any more questions, but she didn't have any doubts that he wasn't in the best of moods when they were shooed out of the kitchen to go for a ride. He drove to his trailer where he was all proper and polite about showing her to a bedroom to change into jeans and boots.

"He asked for it," she whispered as she checked her reflection in the floor-length mirror attached to the back of the door in the small bedroom and adjusted the shoulders of her T-shirt. A twin-sized bed and a desk filled up the room. A picture of LaNita lazing in a lawn chair on the deck was on the desk. Suddenly her mood went from almost cocky to angry. Why was she his Thanksgiving date anyway? LaNita could have flown in for the afternoon and sat beside him at the table.

She jumped when he knocked on the door. "You ready in there?"

She slung the door open and glared at him. "How dare you push that storytelling business off on me."

"How dare you call me a jerk."

"What is her picture doing here? If we're dating, get rid of it."

"We're not really dating, are we?"

She exhaled loudly. "Are we going riding or not?"

A grin split his face and he reached through the door and wrapped her in his arms. Using his fist, he tilted her chin back and kissed her. If she'd wanted to run there would have been no place to go. Two steps back and she'd be falling in a bed; two forward and all she'd run into was more of Kyle's broad chest.

"You are jealous of LaNita," he whispered when he ended the kiss.

"If I was really your girlfriend, I would be," she admitted, then wished she had bitten her tongue off rather than admit that.

"Let's go riding and forget about LaNita, but I'll put the picture away first."

"Just like that? You're going to let me win?"

"No, but someone might run in to use the bathroom or get something to drink from the fridge while they're all out picking up pecans. The trees aren't a hundred yards from the trailer. If I'm going to keep ahead of their dating services I'll have to be careful. I'll make you out to be the best thing since ice cream on a stick and they'll be happy."

She stuck her tongue out at him.

He didn't saddle up horses in the barn but rather hopped on a four-wheeler, slid forward, and padded the room behind him. "Ever ride a mule?"

"I thought we were going on horses. I was going to surprise you by being able to ride. And why do you call that thing a mule?"

"Because it's like a mule. Hearty. Actually does the job and has a better attitude than a mule. Hop on and I'll surprise you instead. We're going to the back of the property to watch the sunset. How's that for romantic? I'll make it sound even better when I tell Lizzy about it tonight after I take you home," he said.

She slung a leg over the machine and propped her hands on the seat beside her. At least she did until he reached down, grabbed her arms, and wrapped them around his middle.

The four-wheeler made enough noise to raise the dead, but she loved the wild ride from the moment he revved it up and hit the gas. Cool afternoon wind swept her hair away from her face. She enjoyed the freedom and the speed. He drove so fast down nothing more than a cow trail that at times, she sucked air. When he braked under a big hackberry tree, she was sorry the trip was over.

He opened the storage compartment under the seat and brought out a blanket, a six-pack of Coke, and a small paper bag. "Isn't this the prettiest place in the world?"

"It's so remote. How far are we from people?"

"Two miles back to my place. Two over to my folks. Probably six that way"—he pointed toward the west—"and a couple over that way"—he pointed in the opposite direction.

A good place to find a rock and do him in, and she might have if he hadn't promised to get rid of that picture of LaNita. She didn't give a tinker's dam if it was because of his family not believing his story. It would be out of his sight too, and that brought her happiness.

Why? she asked herself. She didn't want to answer the question so she avoided it by sitting down on the blanket he'd spread out.

"I'm taking a nap. Want to join me?" he asked.

"You are asking me to sleep with you?" she teased.

"Yep, I am. Sleep, as in shut your eyes and snore. Nothing more. I ate too much dinner and I'm thinking it'll be at least four hours until sunset. We can catch a nap, talk awhile, and then watch it before I take you home."

She removed her boots and stretched out beside him. A squirrel played in the tree above them and she watched it for a while, but soon the heavy meal and warm sun took their toll and she dozed. While they both snoozed clouds rolled in from the southeast. Big black thunderheads so low to the ground, it looked as if a person could reach up and get a handful of them. Lightning zigzagged across the sky and thunder rolled, quietly at first and then louder and louder. At one point she groaned in her sleep, and he instinctively gathered her into his arms and hugged her close without either of them waking up.

The first big drops of rain made the leaves above them shake and still they slept. In a few minutes the sky opened up and great gray sheets of rain fell. They awoke with a start, already half drenched by the time she tugged on her boots and he collected his bearings.

He yelled above the storm for her to leave the blanket and other things and get out from under the tree. She wasted no time obeying. They jumped on the four-wheeler at the same time. She didn't need him to show her where her hands belonged. She wrapped them firmly around him and laid her head against his back, the rain falling so hard it stung her face. He wiped the water from his eyes, got a bead on the pathway, and headed toward home at a much slower speed than he had driven before. Lightning struck a tree behind them. The sound made her scream. Thunder rolled from the clouds so close Greta could have sworn they were driving through them rather than under them. And cold didn't begin to describe the storm. Cold wind whipped down from the north and a few hailstones the size of BBs rattled off the metal fenders.

He parked the machine in the front yard and they ran into the trailer. "Go straight to the bathroom and get a warm shower," he said.

She stood just inside the door, dripping water on the carpet, shivering and wondering just what she was supposed to do for clothing when she did warm up in a shower.

"Go." He pointed. "There's a big blue robe on the hook behind the door. Wrap up in that when you get warm. Leave the water running and I'll get in when you are finished."

She stood under the water for five full minutes before she stopped shaking. Then she washed her hair with his shampoo. A stack of oversized towels waited on the vanity. She dried quickly and wrapped the robe around her body. He waited on the other side when she opened the door. Wearing nothing but a pair of wet jeans, water still running from his hair into his eyes, he stepped past her and shut the door.

She cuddled under a fuzzy throw she found on the sofa and towel-dried her hair. It would be frizzy, but right then she was just glad to have the trailer house walls between her and the storm still raging outside. The phone rang on the table right beside her elbow. Without thinking she picked up the receiver.

"Hello?"

"Greta, this is Kay. I'm just making sure you two are not out in this storm. It came up in a hurry. I was afraid you were up at the backside of the property on the mule," Kay said.

"We were, but we made it home in one piece," Greta said.

"Good. Won't keep you. See you later." Kay hung up.

Home?! Now where did that word come from? She wasn't at home. Far from it.

The phone rang again. She picked it up.

"Hello?"

"Is Kyle there?" a woman's voice asked.

"He's in the shower," Greta said.

"Who is this?"

"Who is this?" she asked right back. Then she felt guilty. It was probably Kelsey's mother with some news about the youth group.

"This is LaNita. I was just calling to talk to Kyle. Who did you say this is?"

"This is Greta Fields," she said.

"Well, I'm finally glad to talk to you, girl. Kyle has talked so much about you since that night I met you in the police station. He likes you, you know," LaNita said.

"No, I didn't," Greta said.

"Whoops! Didn't mean to let the cat out of the bag. Don't tell him I said that. Tell him I have a surprise and I'll call later this week. Bye now."

Greta stared at the phone for several moments and the operator started her mechanical message about hanging up to make a call before she replaced the receiver.

"Did I hear the phone?" Kyle asked from the hallway.

He wore old gray sweatpants and a T-shirt that strained over his chest muscles. Water droplets still hung onto his light brown hair. Greta couldn't find one thing wrong, not even with the long toes on his feet.

"Your mom called. She wanted to make sure we were out of the weather. LaNita called and said she had a surprise to share with you later this week."

He sat down and dragged half the throw away from

her feet to cover his own. "Don't hog the throw, lady. Give me half of it at least. It may be spring before I'm warm again."

"What kind of news does LaNita want to share?"

"Who knows. I threw all your clothes in the dryer. Soon as this lets up I'll take you home."

"Oh, no you don't. I was promised a sunset and you will provide one or else something else as spectacular. Do you own a copy of *P.S. I Love You*?"

He snarled his nose and groaned. "Not a chick flick."

"From the looks of that sky I won't get a sunset so you have to entertain me someway. Your momma will be thinking we fought if I don't stay awhile. This date isn't over until bedtime so I want a movie."

"Okay," he agreed. "And afterward you have to watch Sunday night football with me."

"Agreed. I love football. Who's playing?"

"The Cowboys."

"Then you are on. I'll share the throw but you only get half. Don't be thinking you'll get it all."

He went to the television and found the movie she wanted to watch. By the time he got back to the sofa she had exactly half the throw on his end. He curled his feet up and touched hers before he tucked the covers tightly around both. If she wanted a chick flick then she could warm his feet while she watched it.

Sparks flew and her feet felt as if they were on fire, but she wasn't about to jerk them back. He wouldn't win. But all through the movie she fought the urge to toss common sense out the door and wrap her arms around him.

However, that kind of thing only happened in the movies, not in Murray County, Oklahoma, where reality lived and breathed instead of fairy tales.

Chapter Fourteen

Wilma laid the job application on Greta's desk and waited. The little room where she'd put Greta all those weeks ago hardly looked the same. Boxes upon boxes had been emptied, files entered into the database and repacked orderly before they were sent back to the storage room. Not every single file had been finished but more was done than Wilma ever hoped to have done in four short months.

Finally Greta typed the last few sentences of the report and looked up. "What is this?"

"It's an application for my job. You know I'm retiring at the end of next month and I know this is your last week to work for me."

Greta ignored the paper. "But I'm going back to Tulsa.

I've never said I wanted to stay in this place so why would I apply for your job?"

"Because I want you to do it. I've already written a letter of recommendation and the committee will view all applicants before they make a decision. It's not really my decision but I want your name in the pot. There is no one I'd rather see behind my desk."

Greta held up her fingers. "Thank you, Wilma. But number one, this is a small town. They're going to hire someone they know." Her thumb folded.

"Number two, politics. Someone is going to know someone. I know you but other than that, my name means nothing." The forefinger joined the thumb.

"Number three, I'm here on community service. They'll look at that record and say I shouldn't be working for the city." The middle finger folded.

Greta stared at the two remaining fingers. "Number four."

"Four, Kyle. Five, regret," Wilma finished for her. "Do an old woman a favor. Fill out the application and see what happens."

Greta picked up a pen and wrote her name in the first empty space. "As a favor to you, I'll do it."

Wilma patted her on the shoulder. "That's all I ask."

She finished the application, took it in to Wilma, and promptly forgot all about it. Her goal before she left on Wednesday at eight o'clock was to get the last data entered on the file she had opened so she'd leave nothing unfinished. Doing that would take all of her time and energy for the next three days.

At eight o'clock Kyle tapped on the door frame and she held up a finger, suddenly remembering doing the same thing earlier. One, two, three, but the most important one was four, and that was Kyle. Oh, number five played a big part, yes it did. Regret. Even if they offered her the job tomorrow she couldn't take it. After four incredible weeks of getting to know Kyle better and better, it had to be a clean cut. She couldn't bear to stay and then regret the decision only to break his heart when she left again.

"Sonic?" he asked when she shut down the computer.

"Taco Mayo?"

"Want to compromise and have Braums? My stomach isn't going to handle Mexican tonight," he said.

"How about we go to the lodge and have leftover chicken and dumplings, then?" she said.

He nodded.

Two more days. Tuesday and then Wednesday. Two more evenings of what had evolved as routine semi-dating. He picked her up at noon each day. They both worked eight hours and then had supper together. Sometimes at a fast-food restaurant. Most of the time in the lodge kitchen eating leftovers. Just two more days and then they'd shake hands and say good-bye like adults. That's what they'd agreed on all those weeks ago and nothing had changed. She still wanted to go home. He wasn't leaving Sulphur.

The lodge was empty and Etta had gone to Roxie's place. That too had become routine. They always had their time on the porch if the weather permitted. If not, they'd sit in the dining room, pull the drapes, and watch the rain. Life was not going to pass them by in their later years, according to Etta.

Greta and Kyle each filled a bowl with reheated dumplings and shared a partial loaf of French bread.

"So why is your stomach yucky? You're not catching something now at holiday time, are you?" Greta asked.

"No, just had a bad case right at closing today. Found the body of a homeless man in the park. Curled up under the table on Travertine. He'd been dead awhile," Kyle said.

"Sorry I asked. Think about something else. Have your mom and dad left yet for Austin?"

"This morning bright and early. Momma can't let Mary get all the glory for the dinner on Thursday. Besides Lizzy has a dance recital tonight."

Greta looked across the table. "Oh?"

"Just because we live in small-town America, doesn't mean we are only a notch up from the cavemen. Both of my sisters were dancers as well as barrel racers and rodeo queens."

"What kind of dance?" she asked.

"Ballet. Took lessons right here in town. Momma made noises one year about making me take lessons. I pitched a fit. The boys in school would have never let me live that down. Dad backed me and said if I didn't want to dance I didn't have to. Then he took me to the living room and taught me to two-step. Told Momma that's all the dancing lessons I'd need."

"Hmmm," she mumbled.

He pushed back from the table. "I hate to eat and run but I've got my folks' chores to do plus mine, and it looks like it could start raining any minute."

"I'll walk you to the door."

He kissed her on the top of the head. "Finish your meal. I can let myself out. See you tomorrow."

And he was gone. She missed the steamy good-night kiss, but maybe Kyle knew best. A few more nights of sophomoric kisses at the front door and she'd be tossing common sense in the garbage can and begging him to marry her the next day.

She rinsed their dishes and put them in the dishwasher. It was only a quarter to nine and she had lots to do in the next couple of days.

"Yeah, right," she muttered.

The junkyard dealer was coming the next day to get her car, but she didn't have to be there for that. The repair estimate had proven that she had indeed totaled it so the insurance company had sent her a check last week. It wasn't enough to buy another new sports car but if she was very careful, it would pay for a dependable used one. She'd phoned about insurance rates only to find that she'd be paying high risk for the next four years. That meant she had to buy a pre-owned automobile, pay for it in full, and carry only liability insurance.

"Oh, the joys of adulthood," she said aloud as she pulled her heavy heart up to her room. It hadn't changed since the first time she set foot inside it, but Greta had. She'd found that she could be independent. That wearing clothing from a woman she'd despised wouldn't kill her and neither would hard work. That doing a job well and accomplishing something important, even though it paid nothing in real money, brought satisfaction and self-respect.

She threw herself down on the bed, facing the ceiling and seeing nothing. Rosy and Trey were very happy. She'd admit defeat on that one. Trey had truly found his calling at the college and his heart on Cahill Ranch. Rosy beamed with contentment and loved Trey so much that it made Greta jealous.

Speaking of which, LaNita hadn't called in several weeks. Or if she did, Kyle hadn't mentioned it. And yes, during the soul-searching truth-telling, she would admit she was jealous of the supermodel that had let people think she'd eloped with Kyle.

In self-defense, to keep from falling into a miry depression, her mind skipped to Tulsa and what would be going on there. Time to gear up for a very different lifestyle. To get ready for the holiday parties the next month.

Greta's mother had phoned once a week and the conversations had been tense at best, but she had offered to allow Greta to move into their home until she could find a job. Even that had limitations though. She had exactly two months to find a job and by the end of January she had to have found her own apartment.

It was back to parties and Prada instead of fast food and work boots. Among it all she'd be submitting résumés and doing a lot of praying that she'd find something that would pay for a decent apartment in a nice part of town.

"Hey, Greta, you home?" Jodie's voice carried up the stairs.

She yelled but kept staring at the ceiling. "In my room."

"Where's Kyle?"

"Had to go home and do chores in the dark. Fed him supper and sent him on his way," Greta said.

Jodie pulled the rocking chair up close to the bed and propped her sock feet on the edge of the quilt. "Well, I'm in a dilemma and I got to make a decision by tomorrow. Care to listen?"

"Sure," Greta said. Who'd have thought four months ago that she and Jodie would share anything? Much less friendship?

"The National Championship Rodeo Association called me awhile ago and . . . Do you know anything at all about rodeo or bull-riding?"

"Not one thing, but I can listen. Why would they call you?"

"Because three out of the last five years I've been the top female bull rider in the country. Anyway bull riding is the new thing. The fastest-growing sport, right in there with football and NASCAR. It's predicted in the next five years it will hold its own in the world of sports. So everyone is jumping on the bandwagon early in case they can make a dollar out of it. You ever heard that old country song, "I Was Country When Country Wasn't Cool"? Well, that's where I am right now. I rode bulls back when it wasn't the "in" thing and now that it is I'm one of the few women who've been in the business a long time."

"Go on." Greta sat up.

"Fox News featured PBR, that's Professional Bull Riders, for the second year in its fall sports lineup last September. Came right in behind the NFL and that's really big. Anyway, the new season kicks off in January and I got this call from the *Associated Press.* They're assigning a man to follow the season and are coordinating with the PBR for the in-depth story."

"That's good news, right?" Greta said.

"Yes, for the PBR, but . . ."

"What?"

"I'd decided to get back into the action this year and make the rounds. They want to send the writer with me on the whole rounds. I've still got money saved from the last time I won the title and I can afford to take a big chunk of time away from the ranch. And I'm not so sure I'll be at my best if I'm being tailed all the time by some panty-waist writer from the big city."

"So what are you going to do?"

"Hope like hell he's good-looking since I'll have to look at him for at least four months. The association is going to pick up the expenses if I travel with this fancy-pants writer," Jodie sighed.

"What if he is a she? What makes you think this writer is male?"

"With a name like James Moses Crowe, I'd sure hope it is a male."

Greta giggled. "Don't be too rough on the old boy. He's probably sixty years old, has fifteen grandchildren, is baldheaded, and has a beer gut. Nobody in our generation named their kids James Moses. He'll probably stay in his motel room every night messing with a laptop. Stop worrying."

"You want to come along as my assistant?"

"Are you serious?" Greta asked.

"No, I really can't offer you a job and you'd be miserable. Think about how you hated this place the first month. Multiply that times a million and you'll have a bull-riding tour."

"No thanks, then." Greta fell back on the bed.

"Now, what's going on with you and Kyle?"

"Nothing. A few kisses and an adult decision that we are going to part company on Thursday night like adults. No tears. No regrets. Get on with our lives."

"No broken road bringing you to this place after all, huh?"

"No, and no possibility of taking him with me, either."

"Kind of makes you wish you could be impulsive like a kid instead of sensible like an adult, don't it?"

"Amen," Greta said.

Chapter Fifteen

Thanksgiving morning arrived with a bitter cold north wind straight from Iceland according to Etta. Wind and rain that cold couldn't have been born anywhere else in the world. But no matter what the weather was doing outside Cahill Lodge, cooking, warmth, and wonderful aromas were inside.

Etta and Greta worked together making a traditional meal to be served at five o'clock that evening to Greta and Kyle, Bob and Joann, and all four of their children, including in-laws and grandchildren and Greta's parents. By midmorning, Etta had a ham in one oven, a turkey in the other, and was busy starting side dishes: potato salad, twice-cooked sweet potatoes, orange-cranberry sauce, and the list went on and on. She'd made pies and cakes the day before while Greta finished her last day of community service.

Greta peeled carrots for a relish tray. "Etta, I've got a problem."

"Kyle Parsons?"

"No, not really. We both know what we're going to do about each other. It's my parents. I haven't seen them since Trey and Rosy's wedding. Talked to Mother on the phone but even that was tense. I don't know how to act when they arrive," she said.

"It's not hard to bear a grudge or be mad when you're more than a hundred miles apart. It's a little more difficult when you're in the same room with the person. Your dad will be all right once he gets here. Don't worry. Just be yourself," Etta said.

"But I'm not so sure they'll like who I am now and I'm really not so sure I'm ready for this whole holiday thing I'm about to be plunged into," she said.

"It's like riding a bicycle. It'll all come right back to you. Look at Rosy. She was gone from ranching for four years. Took it up like second nature when she came back home. You'll do the same with your life in Tulsa."

"I hope so. I miss it. I really do."

"Who are you trying to convince, child. Me or you?" Etta's eyes twinkled.

Greta smiled finally. "It's been an experience. Maybe I am trying to convince myself. I am confused. That's a fact."

"You going to tell Kyle you are confused?"

"No, ma'am!" Greta said.

Kyle poked his head into the kitchen. "Tell me what?"

Etta pointed toward the lounge. "Go watch the Macy's parade and leave the cooking to the experts. And Greta, you take him a glass of iced tea. Might as well sit awhile and visit with him. I've got things covered in here."

Greta handed him the glass and sat down on the other end of the sofa. "Want a sandwich to hold you over until supper time?"

"Had a late breakfast so I'm good until we eat," he said.

"I'm nervous about all this," she said.

"I promise I won't pick my nose or use my shirt-sleeve for a napkin. I'll use my best manners. I even got out the *Manners for Dummies* book last night and read up on how to impress a girl's family. It says to be nice to the mother and shake hands firmly with the father, and to clean all the cow manure from under my finger-nails before coming to the table. I got that covered. I even used cologne," he teased.

"Not that. I'm not ashamed of you," she said.

"Let's see. I think you spilled lemonade all over my white shirt and called me a redneck the first time we met at Trey and Rosy's reception. Then you acted like I was something you stepped in out at the hog lot when you wrecked your car. Methinks maybe you have been ashamed of me in the past. Did I use cologne for nothing?"

She swatted at him. He grabbed her hand and pulled

her close for a quick kiss. Just before it ended, his cell phone began to ring. He fished it from the pocket of the jacket he'd tossed on a rocking chair.

"Hello. This is Kyle Parsons."

She waited. Surely the force wouldn't call him in on a holiday. It was his year to be off on Thanksgiving and work on Christmas Eve. She knew because she'd helped Wilma make the schedule on the first day of the month.

"I'll be right there. Take a long, hot shower and when I get there I'll make you hot chocolate and we'll talk this through," he said.

Greta widened her eyes and cocked her head to one side.

He put on his jacket and held out a hand. "Can't stay. Guess I did waste cologne after all. I might not be back for supper so I guess this could be the final good-bye, Greta. I think we agreed on a handshake."

"Who was that?"

"Remember when LaNita called that day it rained on us? She phoned later in the evening to tell me she was getting married the first week in January and I'm supposed to be one of the ushers. I'd offered to work both Christmas Eve and Christmas so I could be off for a week. She was planning a wedding in Australia."

"What's that got to do with today?"

"She caught her groom kissing another woman last night. She threw her engagement ring at him and flew to Oklahoma City. She's out at my house and she's crying. I've got to go."

She shook his hand without a word, the lump in her throat so big she couldn't swallow past it, the stone in her heart aching so bad she thought she would die, and the void in her soul so vast she felt empty. She went to her room, shut the door, and wept.

Greta's parents arrived at four-thirty. Everyone else was already there. Jodie and Rosy both asked about Kyle but Greta brushed it off with a glib answer about being called in to work. No one questioned her answer. Like Etta had prophesized, when Greta was in the room with her parents, she became her old self. At least on the outside. No one knew the turmoil wrecking havoc in her heart.

At eight o'clock Vance and Dianna Fields made the right comments and thanked Roseanna for inviting them for dinner with the family. Greta picked up one suitcase and a garment bag and followed them to their Cadillac. That alone was a severe downsizing from the limo and driver they'd had for years and years.

"You are awfully quiet," Dianna said as they drove north out of town.

"Got a lot to think about," Greta said.

"I talked to Jeffrey Adams last week on the golf course," Vance said. "He said he has a place for you at his firm. Monica needs a secretary. Says she forgets appointments, presentations, and takes three-hour lunches. Remind you of anyone?"

"Guess it does. Thank you, but no thanks. I'll find

my own job, Father. I appreciate you and Mother giving me a place to live until I do. I have an education and I'm not totally stupid. I survived the past four months on my own so I suppose I can find a job."

Vance lifted his chin and looked at her through the rearview mirror. "Without a vehicle?"

"I have the insurance money from the one I wrecked. I can't afford full coverage on a new car so I'll buy a used compact that gets good mileage and insure it for liability only."

"Is this Greta I'm hearing?" Vance laughed.

"It's Greta," she said. *With a broken heart and a brain that keeps telling me I just made the biggest mistake of my life.*

A week later she'd been to four parties. Monica had insisted she come to work at Adams Corporation but Greta had stood firm in her refusal. She hadn't had time to shop for a car and Kyle had not called.

Two weeks later she'd been to four more parties. Monica was so mad she was barely speaking to her. She still hadn't shopped for a car and Kyle had not called.

The next week she canceled all social invitations and bought a 1999 Chevrolet S-10 pickup truck. A one-owner vehicle with low mileage. Then she visited the unemployment office and went to the storage facility where all her things were stored. Sitting on a red leather sofa and staring at box after box of shoes and clothing, bewilderment covered her like a funeral shroud. One step at a time. First a job. After that an apartment, and then she could move all the boxes and furniture, one pickup load at a time. She'd feel more like herself when she was surrounded by her own things.

She picked up a throw pillow and talked to it. "Why didn't he call? I'm his friend as much as LaNita is. He just pretend-married her. He dated me. At least for a little while."

The pickup looked strange sitting in the circular driveway beside a Cadillac. Anyone spying on the Fields household would most likely think the gardener had stayed the night in the old limo driver's apartment over the garage. That gave Greta an idea as she walked through the double front doors into the foyer.

"Suzy, where is Mother?" she asked her mother's secretary, a thin woman dressed in a classy pantsuit, high heels, and pearls.

"In the kitchen. Oh, there was a call for you, Miss Greta. I wrote the number down on the notepad over there." Suzy pointed toward the oak foyer table.

Greta picked up the pad. It was a 580 number with a 622 prefix. That was Sulphur. She picked up the house phone and punched the numbers. She held her breath, hoping Kyle answered.

"Sulphur City Hall, Wilma speaking," the voice said.

Greta's heart fell.

"Hello? Who is this?" Wilma asked.

"Hi, Wilma, this is Greta."

"Answer the phone next time someone says hello to you. How are things going in Tulsa?"

"They're fine. And with you?"

"Not so good. You were right. Remember the number one, two, and three thing you did with your fingers? We've been through one because the committee all knew her; she lasted three days. Two was hired because her daddy is a prominent banker; she lasted three hours. I'm calling to offer you the job. I've been authorized."

"But, Wilma, I can't come back down there."

"Can't or won't? He's moping around, going through the phases after a death. I forgot what they all are, but he's in the numb stage right now. Come home where you belong, girl."

Greta felt a twinge like someone gave her a powerful shot of antibiotic straight into an ailing heart. "I've been to the unemployment office here, just today. They said with my credentials there should be no problem finding a job as soon as the holidays are over. And this has nothing to do with Kyle Parsons or about him."

"I can hold it a week, girl. Any more and they'll run another one in here for me to fire."

"Why hasn't he called me?" Greta asked.

"Why haven't you called him?" Wilma asked right back.

"I can't."

"You got a week. Let me know something next Monday morning. I even talked them into letting you work his hours and that wasn't an easy thing to do, I'm here to tell you. Did you buy a car yet or do I need to send someone to bring you back home?"

"I bought a little S-10 truck this morning," Greta said.

"Then I'll see you at noon next Monday morning." Greta could hear Wilma smiling over the phone.

"Don't hold your breath," Greta grouched.

"Oh, I won't. Don't need to, honey."

"What about LaNita?"

"What about her? You want to know about his personal life, you ask him. You need to know anything about this job, you call me."

Greta replaced the phone and literally ran into her mother when she turned around. "I'm so sorry," she apologized.

"Who were you talking to? Did you already find a job? And whose truck is that in our driveway?"

"I was talking to Wilma, my boss from the police station in Sulphur. She offered me a job but I'm not taking it. I don't belong in a small town. The truck is mine. I bought it and six months worth of liability insurance today. I applied for jobs through the unemployment agency. I checked the storage unit. As soon as I have a job, I'll move out. Do you think Father would rent me the small apartment above the garage?"

"No, he would not. That's not the kind of place for you and that truck has to go, Greta. I'll talk to your grandparents. Grandmother will buy you a decent car and personally, I'm thinking you need to visit a therapist. I told your father it wasn't a good idea to leave you down there among those people that long but he was so angry that you'd wrecked another car."

"Trey was one of those people, Mother," Greta said.

Dianna smoothed the front of her slim skirt and readjusted the matching black wool jacket. The diamonds on her fingers caught the reflection of the crystals in the chandelier hanging right above them in the foyer. "That's not the life for you, Greta. You'd die in that place if you had to stay more than a few months. You've always been a social butterfly. Someday you'll find someone on the right side of the fence and—"

"What are you talking about? I'm as tough as Trey," Greta protested.

"I'm not explaining this so well, am I? Well, suffice it to say, you are back in your father's good graces and you will not be moving out to the chauffeur's apartment. Besides, there's been a merger in the past four weeks. We are planning to use that apartment for what it was intended. I'll be interviewing chauffeurs beginning next week."

"Want my résumé?"

"Don't be cute. You have an hour to get ready for the Christmas tea at the club this afternoon."

"Don't treat me like a child, Mother. I'm not going to the tea."

"Aha! The indifference leaves and argumentativeness begins. Now my daughter is really home."

"No, she's not. She doesn't even know where that is anymore," Greta whispered.

Chapter Sixteen

Greta dressed carefully in a black spaghetti strap Armani gown; a slit up the side to the knee to show off Prada shoes with Austrian crystals embedded in the three-inch spike heels. The hairdresser had swept her black hair up into a bed of loose curls and secured them with a gold clasp adorned with sparkling crystals. When Greta touched up her makeup she remembered the day she'd spent with Kelsey and the girls at Dillard's getting makeovers.

"That was yesterday. Like Mother said I'll get over it," she said and tried to smile, but it came out more a grimace.

Suzy rapped on the open bedroom door. "Your date is here, Miss Greta. James Barton. Fine-looking young man in his tux."

233

"Thank you, Suzy." Greta swept out past her and paused just briefly at the top of the stairs. James was a handsome man in his black tails and bowtie. She wondered if Jodie had met James Moses Crowe yet. Was he a good-looking cowboy in tight Wranglers or a balding older man with fat jowls?

James held out a hand when she reached the bottom step. "You certainly are lovely this evening."

She put on her fake grin. "And you are very handsome, but then you were always pretty. Even when we were in kindergarten."

"Don't be dragging up memories of me back that far. Seriously, Greta, I'm so glad you are back where you belong."

It was on the tip of her tongue to say, "Me too." But she couldn't force the words from her mouth. She would get over it but it wasn't going to be instantaneous. She handed him a silver chinchilla cape to drape around her shoulders. "Why, thank you, James."

The party was at the country club and hosted by the Adams family. Monica wore bright red velvet with a matching floor-length hooded cape trimmed in black mink. At just over five feet, blond-haired, bright green eyes, her entrance stopped conversations as much as Greta's had only moments before. She untied the cape and as it fell from her shoulders her escort handed it off to the nearest paid help. Ignoring the whole process she swept across the room to Greta's side.

"Darling, I'm so glad you came tonight. I've decided to forgive you for turning down Father's offer to be my secretary. Last week's parties were dull without you. Have you gotten over that terrible flu?" Monica asked.

"Flu?"

"It's no sin to be sick, Greta. Dianna told us that you'd been under the weather ever since you came home from the wilderness. You probably contacted some horrible disease from those people. I don't see how Trey stays down there. Did you hear the latest? Julia is really, really engaged and they're planning this big wedding. The honeymoon is going to be in Australia. Why would anyone want to go to the Outback for a honeymoon, but I understand he's from that place and is so rich it makes us all look like white trash."

Australia? Did LaNita and her fiancé make up?

"Whatever were you thinking," Monica rattled on, "you looked like you saw a ghost. Are you sure you're well from the flu?"

"No, I'm still feeling the effects. I think I'll get a glass of wine and find a corner to sit down for a spell," Greta said.

"I'm going to grab Raymond by the arm and dance every single dance tonight. You aren't avoiding me, are you? I am forgiven for my little fit?"

"I'm not avoiding you," Greta said.

"Good. Call me next week. We'll do lunch and catch up on the rest of the news." She disappeared in the crowd.

James was instantly at her elbow. "Dance?"

"Maybe in a minute. Excuse me. I'm going to the powder room."

"I'll save the next one, then," James said.

She sat on a velvet-cushioned bench in front of an enormous mirror and touched up perfect makeup while she remembered the day she'd showered in Kyle's tiny little bathroom. She shut her eyes and inhaled deeply trying to conjure up the aroma of his shampoo. When she couldn't tears filled her eyes, blended with mascara and ran down her cheeks in great black streaks. She picked up a pink washcloth and dabbed at the mess.

"I can't do this," she said. "I cannot live in one world and crave the other. I've got to get over it. I have to or I'm going to be insane before I find a job."

Kyle picked up the phone and dialed the number he'd gotten from Roseanna. That alone had taken all the courage he could muster. He'd given Greta almost three weeks to call him. On Thanksgiving, he'd honestly planned to go home, calm LaNita, and go back to the lodge before Greta left. That's why it had been so easy to shake her hand and walk away. But then things fell apart. LaNita stayed until five o'clock and even then he'd thought he still had time to at least make it back to eat dessert with Roxie and explain things to Greta. Not that he relished the idea of walking away from her, but they'd agreed and he wouldn't be the one to break the rules. They were adults. He'd shake her hand one more time and forget about her.

At least that's what he'd told himself as he started out the door when the phone rang. He had rushed to it, hoping that Greta was willing to make the first move and tell him she didn't want to leave, but it was only the dispatcher at the police station. He'd said there were cows on the road coming into town and if they weren't gathered into the pasture, there could be an accident. He'd put on warmer clothing, had gotten out the four-wheeler, and taken care of that problem. It was eight-thirty when he'd made it back to the lodge and he'd missed Greta by thirty minutes. Etta had said there was still food in the kitchen and she was so sorry he'd been called back to work. His heart had taken a dive down into his cowboy boots and hadn't risen up since.

That was three weeks ago.

The phone rang four times before someone answered. "Fields residence," the lady said.

"May I please speak to Greta?" Kyle asked.

"She's not here at the present time. Could I take a message?"

"When will she be returning?" Kyle asked.

"The party won't be over until late, I'm sure, then she and James may have breakfast somewhere. It might be best if you call tomorrow. I could give her a message if you'd like."

"No thank you. No message."

Kyle gently replaced the receiver.

She'd moved on.

He had no choice but to do the same.

Trees glistened as the bright sun rays bounced off ice-covered limbs, hanging as if they were weeping. Every blade of grass was covered. Clumps of sumac berries hung like Christmas tree ornaments, drooping in the still afternoon. In the shiny, ice-encrusted world, Greta drove carefully. In most places the roads were dry but bridges and shady areas still sported icy patches. The night of the party the temperatures had dropped and a drizzle fell all night. The next day the eastern part of the state was covered. Electricity was down in most places. By Sunday, the roads were clearing but the countryside still looked like it was covered in diamonds.

Monday morning found her inching down the highway going less than forty miles an hour. The farther south she drove the harder she gripped the truck's steering wheel. Her father had declared that she was a fool for taking this job. Her mother had thrown up her hands in disgust and defeat and refused to talk to her. She'd called the man who owned the storage place and asked him if he could recommend anyone for a few hours to help her clean out her unit. He did and she met them there that morning at seven o'clock.

What ifs played through her mind as she drove. What if she was making the biggest mistake of her life? What if she regretted her decision? What if she had another wreck in this God forsaken ice storm? What if her father was right and she was on a fool's trip only to find she wasn't happy with the job?

Her knuckles were white when she made a left turn off the highway and geared the truck down to thirty miles an hour on the back roads, which hadn't had the benefit of a layer of sand. By the time she made the second left her hands were clammy and threatening to slide off the steering wheel. The tree-lined lane was so narrow it was impossible to turn around and go back.

The first thing she saw was a silver car sitting in the driveway beside Kyle's truck. Then LaNita threw open the front door, pulled a black sable coat around her body, and gave Kyle a hug before she headed toward the car. She smiled and waved when she looked up at the big U-Haul truck coming to a stop beside her rental car. She was already backing out of the yard when Greta opened the door and stepped out.

Kyle blinked twice. Was that Greta? He'd wondered who'd gotten lost in this horrible weather and turned down his lane by mistake, but . . . surely that wasn't Greta. He rubbed his eyes. They were blurry for a moment when he opened them and realized that it was Greta and not a figment of his imagination.

"What are you doing here? And what is that?" he asked when she stepped up onto the porch.

She stopped two feet from him. "Nice greeting for someone who hasn't even bothered to call and see if I'm alive."

"Come in before you let out all my heat," he said.

"Thank you," she replied.

She'd made a mistake. In one scenario she'd imagined him opening his arms and planting one of those earth-shaking kisses on her cold lips. In reality, LaNita had just left and probably since she'd been jilted, they'd finally realized they were ready to have a for-real ceremony and really, really tie the knot.

She could have wept.

"I'm sorry. I shouldn't have come without calling. It's just that . . ."

"It's just what, Greta?" he asked hoarsely. She was so beautiful. Even with a red nose and no makeup and her hair tied up in a ponytail, wearing jeans and a sweatshirt.

"Wilma offered me her job and I called her Friday night and said I'd be at work at noon today, and anyway that's in an hour, and Trey said I could use part of one of the barns to keep my things in until I find a place, and Etta said I could stay in my old room at the lodge, and I figured out I'd fallen in love with you and I don't care where I live and . . ."

She sucked in a lungful of air and started to finish but couldn't because he'd wrapped her in his arms and was stopping all talk with one kiss after another. Finally she pushed him away and started again. "And I just realized that LaNita and you have probably figured out that you are meant for each other and I'm sorry I left because I know now I made a mistake because I do love you and it's too late . . ."

He kissed her again, this time longer and more passionately.

"And Kyle, what am I going to do? I can't work in the same place with you if you are married to her and—"

"Shut up, Greta," he rasped and kissed her a third time.

"But . . ."

"LaNita married her fiancé last week in a private ceremony in New York. She's flying to Houston for a photo shoot today and had a layover in Oklahoma City, so she came down to show me the pictures. She's only been here an hour. Did you say you loved me?"

"I did." She made no effort to move out of his arms, knowing it was exactly where she belonged for all eternity.

"And you have to be at work in one hour?"

"I do."

He touched her hair and ran his thumb down her jawline. He wasn't dreaming. She was really here and she said she was staying.

"I love you too," he said.

"Will you take me to work and help me unload that truck afterward?" she asked.

He looked out the window without loosening his hold on her. "Is that a pickup truck I see behind that U-Haul?"

"It's mine. I bought it Friday and paid six months insurance on it."

He grinned. "Welcome home, Greta."

And kissed her one more time.

Chapter Seventeen

The wedding took place three weeks later in the First
Baptist Church of Sulphur on a Friday night. Greta
wore a simple white shantung suit with a straight skirt,
short jacket, and pale yellow silk blouse. She carried a
bouquet of yellow roses tied with wide white ribbon.
The five bridesmaids from her youth group wore their
favorite Sunday school dresses and each carried a single
rose with trailing yellow ribbons. Kyle chose a black
three-piece suit, white shirt, and bolo tie. His grooms-
men, Andy, Jim, Kade, Jason, and Kenny from the youth
group, wore starched jeans and white shirts.

They stood before the preacher in front of family and
friends and repeated their vows. Dianna Fields dabbed at
her eyes during the ceremony. What was it about this
place that claimed both her children? They'd been raised

right, were cultured, well traveled, had been given the right lessons, the right contacts—everything money and love could purchase. And here they were, happy in a town of no more than six thousand people, with no shopping malls, not even a Starbucks.

Vance had offered to give Greta the moon if she'd call off the wedding. When he realized she was serious about her job and her groom, he'd offered to give her a big wedding in Tulsa or the money to elope to France or Italy.

"Thanks, Father, but no thanks. I'll pay for my own wedding and it's going to be in our church with our youth group around us. You and Mother are invited and so are Grandmother and Grandfather. It'll be a very simple affair at the church with a reception at the lodge afterward," she'd said.

"And now I pronounce you man and wife. Kyle, you may kiss your bride," the preacher said.

"I love you," Kyle whispered just before he kissed her.

"And I love you," Greta barely got out before his lips touched hers.

The lodge lobby had been decorated for the reception and sported two long tables covered with finger foods and a round table covered with a lace cloth holding a three-tiered cake Etta and Roxie had insisted on making. Two yellow roses graced the top layer of the Italian crème cake covered with cream cheese icing. A chocolate groom's cake topped with dipped strawberries waited on another table.

The bride and groom refused a formal receiving line, opting instead for an informal reception where they circulated among the guests, visiting with each and every one.

"So you told him to divorce me?" LaNita asked when they stopped at her table.

"I was jealous as hell," Greta whispered in her ear.

LaNita almost choked on laughter. "I'm glad. He deserves someone just like you. He'd run over any other woman."

Kyle slipped his arm around Greta's waist. "Are you two whispering about me?"

Greta kissed him on the end of his nose. "Don't be so egotistical. We were exchanging recipes."

LaNita winked and they moved on.

Vance shook his new son-in-law's hand. "I don't know what you people have down in this part of the state but she's as happy as Trey."

"He loved me," Greta said. "I had a dream that you just flat-out gave me to him because he rode up on a horse and asked for my hand in marriage."

"After that last wreck I might have done just that," Vance chuckled.

"After that last wreck I'm not so sure I'd have asked for her hand," Kyle said.

"But you did in the long run, didn't you?" Greta teased.

"Yes, ma'am," Kyle said.

Roseanna walked up to the couple. "I heard that 'yes, ma'am.' *Now* you learn what to say and when to say it."

"Takes the right woman," Kyle said.

"And don't you ever forget it," Greta teased.

Jodie walked up and hugged them both at the same time.

"So where is James Moses Crowe? When do you leave?" Greta asked.

"He's been replaced by Sawyer Carver. Now doesn't that sound more like my kind of man? Congratulations, you two. I still can't believe you came back, Greta, or that you are married. Be happy." She headed toward the cake table.

Greta's grandfather slipped a check into her hand. "We didn't have any idea what you all might need since Kyle already has a home and Dianna said you were donating part of your furniture to the local library because you couldn't fit it into his house, so we want you to have this. Buy some more land or cows with it. A rancher can always use those things."

She kissed him on the cheek. "Thank you, Grandfather."

Kyle nuzzled her ear. "How much longer do we have to stay?"

"Not one more minute. Hey, all you unmarried women. I'm about to throw this bouquet so line up and let the fight begin," she said.

Kelsey, Sueann, Cathy, Molly, and Amber all fought

for the front line. Jodie and a few of the older unmarried ladies took the back rows.

Greta counted. "One, two, three."

Then she faked a throw.

"That wasn't funny," Kelsey said.

"I know, but this is." Greta strolled across the lobby and handed Jodie the bouquet. "May you be as miserable as I was before I finally admitted defeat and came home where I belonged," she whispered.

"You rat." Jodie laughed. "Be happy, you two."

"We will." Kyle grinned.

"Want me to drive?" Greta teased as they ran through a shower of rice on the way to the truck.

"No, I do not. I don't want you to speed, kill another bull, and us having to spend our honeymoon night in jail," he said as he settled her into the passenger seat of his truck.

"You reckon you can speed, not kill a bull, and get us to the trailer in a hurry?" She raised an eyebrow.

"Yes, ma'am." He fired up the engine and they left the lodge with tin cans rattling behind a truck decorated with *Just Married* written on the back window.